THE FATAL EGGS

THE FATAL EGGS

Mikhail Bulgakov

Translated by Michael Karpelson

TRANSLIT PUBLISHING

Translit Publishing
www.translit.ca

ISBN 978-0-9812695-2-8

Also available in multiple e-book formats (ISBN 978-0-9812695-3-5).

CONTENTS

Biographical Note

Mikhail Afanasievich Bulgakov was born in 1891 in Kiev, the eldest son of a professor at a theological seminary. After graduating from the medical school at Kiev University in 1916, Bulgakov served as a field doctor in the Russian civil war and was eventually transferred to the Caucasus, where he would later decide to pursue a full-time literary career. His brothers enlisted as well, but ended up in Paris, while Mikhail remained in Russia. He began writing around 1916; by 1924, he had completed his first major novel, *The White Guard*.

The Fatal Eggs was first published in 1925 in the journal *Nedra*. Bulgakov faced extensive censorship and criticism for his allegedly anti-Soviet views, and many of his works remained unpublished until long after his death. *The Fatal Eggs*, an early short novel, is the only one of Bulgakov's better known works that was published in its entirety during the author's lifetime. During his life, Bulgakov was best known for his plays, such as *Days of the Turbins*, based on *The White Guard* and rumored to be particularly favored by Joseph Stalin. However, relentless hounding by Soviet critics effectively stifled his writing career by the late 1920s.

In 1930, with all of his plays banned and no theater willing to employ him, Bulgakov wrote to the Soviet government asking for permission to emigrate. Stalin telephoned Bulgakov personally and denied his request, appointing Bulgakov to a position at the Moscow Art Theater instead. During the last decade of his life, Bulgakov continued to work on plays, stage adaptations, and short stories, as well as his best known and final novel, *The Master and Margarita*.

Bulgakov died from inherited nephrosclerosis in 1940, leaving the editing of *The Master and Margarita* unfinished. Today, Bulgakov is considered one of the most important Russian literary figures of the 20th century.

THE FATAL EGGS

TRANSLIT
PUBLISHING

CHAPTER 1

★

CURRICULUM VITAE OF PROFESSOR PERSIKOV

On the evening of April 16, 1928, the professor of zoology at Fourth State University and director of the Zoological Research Institute in Moscow, Persikov, entered his laboratory at the institute, which is on Herzen Street. The professor lit the frosted glass sphere on the ceiling and looked around.

That ill-fated evening should be considered the beginning of the horrifying catastrophe that followed, just as Professor Vladimir Ipatievich[1] Persikov should be considered the root cause of this catastrophe.

He was exactly fifty-eight years old. He had a wonderful, pestle-shaped bald head with tufts of yellowish hair sticking out at the sides. A cleanly shaven face, a protruding lower lip that gave Persikov's face a permanently capricious expression. Small, old-fashioned glasses in silver frames on his red nose; small, sparkling eyes; tall, round-shouldered. Spoke in a screeching, high-pitched, croaking voice, and one of his many eccentricities was shaping his right index finger into a hook and squinting whenever he was speaking confidently and authoritatively. And since he always spoke authoritatively, for his knowledge of his fields of study was absolutely phenomenal, those conversing with Persikov would see the hook quite often. Outside his fields – that is, zoology, embryology, anatomy, botany, and geography – Professor Persikov rarely said anything at all.

1 In Russian, the polite form of address consists of the first name and patronymic.

Professor Persikov did not read the papers or go to the theater, and his wife had left him with a tenor from Zimin's Opera House in 1913, leaving him the following note:

> *"Your frogs make me shudder with intolerable disgust.*
> *I will be unhappy my entire life because of them."*

The professor did not remarry, and he had no children. He was very short-tempered, but bore no grudges. He enjoyed cloudberry tea and lived on Prechistenka in an apartment with five rooms, one of which was occupied by a dry little old lady, the housekeeper Maria Stepanovna, who looked after the professor like a nanny.

In 1919, they took away three of the professor's five rooms. Then he declared to Maria Stepanovna:

"If they don't put an end to this nonsense, Maria Stepanovna, I will leave the country."

Undoubtedly, had the professor carried out his plan, he would have easily been able to find a position in the zoology department of any university in the world, for he was an absolutely first-rate scientist, while in the field dealing with amphibians he had no equal except perhaps for professors William Veckle in Cambridge and Giacomo Bartolomeo Beccari in Rome. The professor could read four languages besides Russian, and he spoke German and French as well as his native language. However, he did not carry out his plan of leaving the country, while 1920 turned out even worse than 1919. Various things happened, one right after the other. Bolshaya Nikitskaya was renamed to Herzen Street. Then the clock built into the wall of the house at the corner of Herzen and Mokhovaya stopped at a quarter past eleven, and afterwards, unable to bear the upheaval of that famous year, eight amazing specimens of tree frogs perished in the institute's terrariums, followed by fifteen ordinary toads, and, finally, an exceptional specimen of the Surinam toad.

Right after the toads' passing had devastated that first order of amphibians that is rightly called tailless, the irreplaceable old caretaker of the institute, Vlas, who did not belong to the class of amphibians, also departed to a better world. The cause of his death, however, was the same as that of the unfortunate amphibians, and Persikov determined it right away:

"Malnutrition!"

The scientist was absolutely right: Vlas needed flour for nourishment, and the toads needed mealworms, whereas after the former vanished, so did the latter. Persikov attempted to transfer the remaining twenty tree frog specimens to a cockroach diet, but then the cockroaches also disappeared, showing their hostile attitude towards military communism. As a result, the final specimens also had to be discarded into the trash pit in the courtyard of the institute.

The effect of the deaths on Persikov, and especially that of the Surinam toad, defied description. For some reason, he placed the entirety of the blame on the People's Commissar of Education.

Standing in his winter hat and galoshes in the hallway of the freezing-cold institute, Persikov spoke to his assistant Ivanov, a most elegant gentleman with a pointed blond beard:

"Killing's too good for him after this, Pyotr Stepanovich! What do they think they are doing? They'll ruin the institute! Eh? An incomparable male specimen of *Pipa americana*, thirteen centimeters in length…"

Later, things got worse. After Vlas's death, the windows in the institute froze completely, such that the frilly ice covered the inside surfaces of the glass. Rabbits, foxes, wolves, fish, and every last grass snake perished. Persikov would remain silent for entire days, and then he contracted pneumonia, but survived. After recovering, he would come to the institute twice a week and, in the round hall, where it was always five below freezing regardless of the temperature outside, deliver a series of lectures entitled "Reptiles of the Torrid Zone," – wearing galoshes, a hat with ear flaps, and a scarf, breathing out white steam – to an audience of eight. The rest of the time, Persikov would lie coughing under a blanket on his couch on Prechistenka, in a room full of books piled up to the ceiling, and stare into the maw of a small furnace, which Maria Stepanovna fueled with gilded chairs, as he reminisced about the Surinam toad.

But everything in this world ends. 1920 and 1921 came to an end, and in 1922, things began to drift in the reverse direction. Firstly, a still young but very promising zoological caretaker Pankrat appeared in place of the late Vlas. Also, the institute began to be heated again. And in the summer, Persikov, with Pankrat's assistance, captured fourteen common toads on the Kliazma River. The terrariums became full of life once more… In 1923, Persikov lectured eight times a week – three times at the institute and five times at the university. In 1924, it was thirteen times a week, not counting the Workers' Faculty[2]. And in 1925, in spring, he distinguished himself by failing seventy six students during exams, all on the subject of amphibians.

"What, you mean you don't know the difference between amphibians and reptiles?" Persikov would ask. "That's just ridiculous, young man. Amphibians don't have metanephros[3]. The metanephros is missing. So there. For shame. You are a Marxist, no doubt?"

"A Marxist," the failed student would reply, fading away.

"Right, please try again in the fall," Persikov would answer politely and then shout spiritedly to Pankrat: "Next!"

Just as amphibians come to life during the first copious rain after a prolonged drought, so did Persikov come to life in 1926, when a joint American-Russian venture built fifteen fifteen-story houses in the center of Moscow, starting at the intersection of Gazetny Lane and Tverskaya, as well as three hundred workers' cottages on the outskirts of the city, each with eight apartments – putting an end, once and for all, to the awful and comical housing shortage that plagued Muscovites from 1919 until 1925.

---

2 *Workers' Faculty* – Soviet educational institutions in the 1920s and 30s, intended to prepare workers and peasants for institutions of higher learning.
3 *Metanephros* – A phase of kidney development.

In fact, it was a truly marvelous summer in Persikov's life, and he would sometimes rub his hands together contentedly and chuckle quietly as he recalled being cooped up in two rooms with Maria Stepanovna. Now he got back his previous five rooms, spread himself out, arranged his two and a half thousand books, his mounted animals, diagrams, and specimens, and lit a green lamp on the desk in the study.

The institute had also changed beyond recognition – they repainted it in cream color, built a special water line to deliver water to the room with the amphibians, replaced all the panes with mirrored glass, provided five new microscopes, glass laboratory tables, 2,000-watt spherical lights, reflectors, and museum cases.

Persikov came to life, and the entire world learned about this the moment his brochure was published in December of 1926:

"More on the reproduction of *Amphineura*, or chitons[4]," 126 pages, "Proceedings of the Fourth State University."

And in the fall of 1927, a definitive work of three hundred and fifty pages, which was translated into six languages, including Japanese: "Embryology of *Pipa*, Spadefoot Toads, and Frogs." Price: 3 rubles. StatePub.

And in the summer of 1928 came the unthinkable, the horrible…

---

4 *Chitons* – A type of primitive marine molluscs.

Chapter 2

★

A Colorful Swirl

And so, the professor lit the glass sphere and looked around. He lit the reflector over the long laboratory table, put on his white coat, jingled some implements on the table…

Many of the thirty thousand motorized coaches that sped around Moscow in 1928 passed through Herzen Street, rustling over the smooth pavestones, and every minute the hum and gnashing of streetcars from the 16th, 22nd, 48th, or 53rd lines could be heard as they rolled off Herzen and onto Mokhovaya. A pale and foggy moon crescent was visible high up and far away, next to the dark and heavy dome of the Church of Christ, casting colorful reflections through the mirrored windows of the laboratory.

But neither the moon nor the hum of springtime Moscow interested Professor Persikov in the least. He was sitting on a three-legged revolving stool, and his tobacco-stained fingers were turning the knob of a splendid Zeiss microscope, presently loaded with an ordinary undyed sample of fresh amoebas. Just as Persikov was switching the magnification from five to ten thousand, the door opened, a pointed beard and leather apron came into view, and his assistant called out:

"Vladimir Ipatievich, I set up the mesentery[1]. Care to have a look?"

Persikov slid down quickly from the stool, left the knob in the halfway position, and walked to the assistant's office, twirling a cigarette slowly in his hands. There, on the glass table, a

---

1 *Mesentery* – A structural membrane in the abdomen.

half-dead frog, numb with fear and pain, had been crucified on a cork mat, while its transparent micaceous innards were draped under the microscope from its bloodied belly.

"Very nice," Persikov said, placing his eye over the microscope's eyepiece.

Evidently there was something very interesting to be seen in the frog's mysentery, where lively blood cells ran down the streams of the vessels, clearly visible, as if on the palm of one's hand. Persikov forgot all about his amoebas and, for an hour and half, took turns looking through the microscope with Ivanov. During this time, the scientists were exchanging spirited words, incomprehensible though they were to mere mortals.

Finally, Persikov pulled away from the microscope and declared:

"The blood is curdling, nothing more to be done here."

The frog moved its head with difficulty, its fading eyes expressing a clear sentiment: "Real bastards, that's what you two are."

Stretching his swollen legs, Persikov got up, returned to his laboratory, yawned, rubbed his perpetually inflamed eyelids, and, sitting down on his stool, he glanced through the microscope. His fingers were already on the knob, and he was about to turn it, but turn it he did not. With his right eye, Persikov saw a blurry white disk full of blurry white amoebas, and in the middle of the disk was a colorful swirl, resembling a woman's curls. Persikov had seen this swirl many times, and so had hundreds of his students, and no one ever paid it any mind, because there was no reason to do so. The colorful ray of light only interfered with observation and showed that the sample was not in focus. As a result, it was always wiped out mercilessly with a single turn of the knob, flooding the field of view with even white light. The zoologist's long fingers had already gripped the knob firmly, but then they trembled and slid off. Persikov's right eye was to blame for this – suddenly, it grew alert, astounded, even alarmed. To the great misfortune of the republic, it was not some untalented mediocrity sitting at the microscope. No, it was Professor Persikov himself! His entire life, his entire mind was now concentrated in his right eye. For five whole minutes, the higher being observed the lower being in stony silence, suffering and straining its eye over the unfocused sample.

Everything around was quiet. Pankrat had already fallen asleep in his room in the vestibule, and only once did the glass ring melodiously and gently in the cabinets – Ivanov was locking up his laboratory as he left. The front door groaned after him. Then came the professor's voice. It is not known whom he was addressing.

"What's this? I don't understand a thing."

A late-running truck passed by on Herzen Street, shaking the old walls of the institute. A flat glass bowl full of tweezers clanked on the table. The professor grew pale and placed his hand over the microscope like a mother protecting her babe from danger. Moving the knob was now out of the question; oh no, Persikov only feared that some outside force would push what he had seen from his field of view.

It was a bright, white morning, and a golden band of light was cutting across the cream-colored entrance of the institute when the professor finally left the microscope and approached the window on numb legs. His trembling fingers pushed a button, and solid black blinds covered the morning, and a wise scholarly night enveloped the laboratory. Sallow and inspired, Persikov spread his legs and said, staring into the parquet floor with watering eyes:

"But how can it be? It's monstrous! It's monstrous, gentlemen," he repeated, turning towards the toads in the terrarium, but the toads were asleep and did not answer.

He was silent for a while, then approached the light switch, raised the blinds, turned off all the lights, and glanced into the microscope. His face tensed, and his tufted yellow eyebrows moved together.

"Mm-hmm, mm-hmm," he grumbled. "It's gone. I see. I see-e-e," he drawled in a mad, inspired voice, glancing at the frosted sphere on the ceiling. "Simple enough."

He lowered the hissing blinds again and lit the sphere. He looked into the microscope, and a happy, almost ravenous grin appeared on his face.

"I'll catch it," he said solemnly and weightily, raising his finger. "I'll catch it. Maybe even from the sun."

The blinds whirled up again. The sun was out. It flooded the walls of the institute and cast slanted rays on the pavestones of Herzen Street. The professor looked out the window, trying to figure out where the sun would be in the daytime. He moved away from the window and back again, as if dancing lightly, and finally lay down on his stomach on the windowsill.

Then he commenced important and mysterious work. He covered the microscope with a glass belljar. He melted a piece of wax over the blue flame of a gas burner and sealed the edges of the belljar to the table, then imprinted his thumb on the wax. He shut off the gas, walked out, and locked the door of the laboratory.

The hallways of the institute were dimly lit. The professor reached Pankrat's room and knocked on the door for a long time without effect. Finally, a rumbling came from behind the door, resembling a chained dog. Then there was coughing and moaning, and Pankrat appeared in a spot of light, wearing striped underpants tied at the ankles. His eyes stared savagely at the scientist, and he was still whimpering softly, half-asleep.

"Pankrat," the professor said, looking at him over his glasses, "I'm sorry I woke you. Listen, my friend, do not go into my laboratory in the morning. I left some work there that cannot be disturbed. Understood?"

"U-u-uh, un-un-understood," Pankrat replied, failing to understand anything. He was swaying and growling.

"No, listen, you have to wake up, Pankrat," the zoologist spoke, jabbing Pankrat lightly in the ribcage, which caused fright to appear on his face and an inkling of comprehension in his eyes. "I locked the laboratory," Persikov continued, "so don't clean it until I return. Understood?"

"Yessir," Pankrat rasped.

"Excellent, now go back to bed."

Pankrat turned around, disappeared in the doorway, and tumbled immediately into his bed, while the professor went to the vestibule to get dressed. He put on his gray summer coat and soft hat, and then, remembering the image in the microscope, he stared at his galoshes for several seconds, as if he were seeing them for the first time. He put on the left one and then tried to put on the right one over top of the left, but it would not fit.

"What a monstrous coincidence, though, that he called me away," said the scientist, "or else I would not have noticed it. But what does this promise us? The devil alone knows what it promises!" The professor grinned, squinted at his galoshes, took off the left one, and put on the right one. "Good lord! I cannot even imagine all the consequences…" The professor prodded his left galosh with contempt, for it irritated him by refusing to fit on top of the right one, and walked towards the exit wearing only one galosh. Here he lost his handkerchief and walked outside, slamming the heavy door behind him. Out on the steps, he searched for matches in his pockets for a long time, patting his sides, and, finding nothing, set off down the street with an unlit cigarette in his mouth.

The professor did not meet a single person all the way until the church. There he raised his head and stared at the golden dome. The sun was licking it sweetly on one side.

"How could I have not seen it before? What a coincidence… Bah, that's dumb," he pondered, leaning down and staring at his differently shod feet. "Hmm… what to do? Go back to Pankrat? No, there's no waking him up now. Shame to throw the damn thing away. I'll have to carry it." He took off the galosh and began to carry it with distaste.

An old car drove out of Prechistenka with three people inside: two drunk men and a woman with gaudy makeup sitting on their lap, wearing those silk pants that were so popular in 1928.

"Hey, daddy-o!" she shouted in a low, hoarse voice. "Why'd you drink away your other galosh?"

"Old man must have got loaded at the 'Alcazar,'" the drunk man on the left howled, while the one on the right stuck his head out the window and shouted:

"Hey pops, is the nightclub on Volkhonka still open? We're headed there!"

The professor looked at them sternly over his glasses, dropped the cigarette from his mouth, and immediately forgot about their existence. A blade of sunlight was working its way through Prechistensky Boulevard, and the dome of Christ the Savior began to burn with light. The sun had emerged.

Chapter 3

★

Persikov's Got It

Here is what happened. When the professor put his brilliant eye to the eyepiece, he noticed, for the first time in his life, that a particularly clear and thick ray of light was standing out in the multicolored swirl. The ray was bright red, protruding from the swirl like a tiny blade, about the size of a needle.

As bad luck would have it, this ray attracted the experienced eye of the prodigy for several seconds.

In it, in this ray, the professor saw something a thousand times more important and significant than the ray itself – that frail offspring born accidentally from the movement of the microscope mirror and objective. Due to the fact that the assistant had called away the professor, the amoebas had spent an hour and a half in this ray, and here is what happened: while, in the disk outside the ray, the grainy amoebas lay weakly and helplessly, strange things were transpiring beneath the sharp red sword. Life boiled in the red band of light. Stretching out their pseudopodia, the amoebas reached for the red band with all their might, and, once in it, they came to life as if by magic. Some unknown force had breathed life into them. They flocked in swarms and fought one another for a place under the ray. Inside the ray, they engaged in furious (for lack of a better word) reproduction. Breaking and overturning all the laws that Persikov knew like the back of his hand, they budded before his eyes with lightning speed. They broke into pieces under the ray, and two seconds later each part became a new, fresh organism. These organisms reached maturity and attained a large size in just a few moments, only to immediately breed a new generation. The red band, and then the entire disk, became crowded, and a struggle inevitably broke out. The newly born tore each other to pieces and consumed the remains. The corpses of those who had perished in the struggle to exist lay among the newborns. The best and the strongest won, and they were horrible. Firstly, they were about twice the size of ordinary amoebas, and secondly, they distinguished themselves with unusual aggressiveness and speed. Their movements were blazing fast, their pseudopodia much longer than normal, and they worked them – without any exaggeration – like a squid works its tentacles.

On the second evening, the pale and haggard professor, who had not eaten and subsisted solely on thick, hand-rolled cigarettes, was studying the new generation of amoebas, and on the third evening he moved on to the source: that is, the red ray.

The gas was hissing quietly in the burner, traffic shuffled along the street outside, and the professor, poisoned by his hundredth cigarette, leaned back on the revolving chair and closed his eyes halfway.

"Yes, it's all clear now. The ray brought them to life. It's a new ray, unexplored and undiscovered by anyone. The first thing I have to determine is whether it only comes from electrical light or from the sun as well," Persikov muttered to himself.

And in the course of another night, he determined it. Persikov captured three rays in three microscopes but failed to obtain anything from the sun, and said this:

"One would assume that it is not present in the solar spectrum… hmm… in other words, one would assume that it can only be obtained from electrical light." He gazed lovingly at the frosted glass sphere above, spent a moment in inspired thought, and then invited Ivanov into his laboratory. He told him everything and showed him the amoebas.

Private docent[1] Ivanov was shocked, completely crushed: how could something as simple as that little red arrow have

---

1 *Private docent* – An academic title in certain European universities, indicating that the holder is qualified to become a tenured professor.

gone unnoticed for so long, may the devil take it! Anyone could have noticed it, even Ivanov himself. And it was truly monstrous! Why, just look…

"Just look, Vladimir Ipatievich," Ivanov spoke, glued to the eyepiece in horror. "Look at what's going on! They are growing before my eyes… Look, look…"

"I have been observing them for three days now," Persikov said passionately.

Then the two scientists had a conversation which can be summarized as follows: private docent Ivanov would undertake to construct, using lenses and mirrors, a chamber where the ray could be produced in magnified form and without the use of a microscope. Ivanov hopes – in fact, he is quite confident – that it would be exceptionally simple. He'll get the ray, Vladimir Ipatievich need not doubt it. Then there was a slight awkwardness.

"When I publish the work, Pyotr Stepanovich, I will mention that you constructed the chambers," Persikov put in, feeling it necessary to resolve the awkwardness.

"Oh, it's not important… but of course…"

And the awkwardness was resolved at once. From that moment on, the ray consumed Ivanov as well. While Persikov, wasting away and growing ever thinner, spent entire days and half the nights by the microscope, Ivanov was fussing around in the brilliantly lit physics laboratory, setting up the lenses and mirrors. A mechanic assisted him.

After a request via the Commissariat of Education, Persikov was shipped three packages from Germany containing mirrors and an assortment of biconvex, biconcave and even some convex-concave polished lenses. In the end, Ivanov did manage to construct the chamber and actually isolate the red ray. And, to do him justice, he did it expertly: the curved ray turned out sharp, strong, and saturated, about four centimeters wide.

On June 1st, the chamber was set up in Persikov's laboratory, and he eagerly began experimenting with frogspawn illuminated by the ray. The experiments produced incredible results. In the course of two days, thousands of tadpoles hatched from the eggs. But that was not all: within just one more day, the tadpoles matured into frogs so vicious and ravenous that half of them were immediately devoured by the other half. The surviving half, however, immediately began to lay eggs, and in two days they bred an absolutely countless new generation without any need for the ray. All hell broke loose in the scientist's laboratory: the tadpoles escaped from the room and crawled all over the institute. Loud choruses of frogs sounded from every corner, both in the terrariums and right on the floor, like in a swamp. Pankrat, who had already feared Persikov like the plague, now felt only one thing: mortal terror. A week later, the scientist himself felt he was going a little crazy. The institute was filled with the smell of ether and potassium cyanide, which almost poisoned Pankrat when he removed his mask at the wrong time. They finally managed to kill off the growing swampland generations with the poisons and air out the laboratories.

Persikov said this to Ivanov:

"You know, Pyotr Stepanovich, the way the ray affects the deuteroplasm[2] and the egg cell in general is phenomenal."

Ivanov, normally a cool and collected gentleman, interrupted the professor in a strange voice:

"Vladimir Ipatievich, why are you talking about these minor details, about the deuteroplasm? Let's speak plainly: you've discovered something extraordinary." It was evidently with great effort, but Ivanov managed to squeeze out the words: "Professor Persikov, you have discovered the ray of life!"

Faint color appeared on Persikov's pale, stubbly cheekbones.

"Well, well, well," he muttered.

"The name you'll make for yourself..." Ivanov continued. "My head is spinning from the mere thought. You see, Vladimir Ipatievich," he continued passionately, "H. G. Wells's heroes

---

2 *Deuteroplasm* – The nutritive substances in an egg cell.

are nothing compared to you... And I thought it was all just fairy tales... Do you remember his *Food of the Gods*?"

"Oh, it's a novel," Persikov replied.

"Right, of course, it's really well known!"

"I forgot about it," Persikov replied. "I remember reading it, but I forgot."

"What do you mean you forgot? Just look," Ivanov reached over to the glass table and picked up a frog of incredible size, with a swollen belly. Even in death, its snout had retained a sinister expression. "It's monstrous!"

CHAPTER 4

★

THE WIDOW DROZDOVA

God knows why – perhaps Ivanov was to blame, or perhaps big news tend to spread right through the air, but only talk about the ray and about Professor Persikov spread suddenly through the enormous, seething city of Moscow. It was only vaguely, in passing, however. News of the miraculous discovery hopped through the shining capital like a wounded bird, taking to the air and then disappearing again, until the end of July, when a short notice about the ray appeared on the twentieth page of the *Izvestiya* newspaper under the heading "Science and technology news." It related dryly that a professor from Fourth University had discovered a ray that could drastically raise the vital functions of lower organisms, and that the discovery would have to be verified. The name was distorted, of course, and read: "Pevsikov."

Ivanov brought the newspaper and showed it to Persikov.

"Pevsikov," Persikov grumbled, fussing around with the chamber in the laboratory. "How do those squealers know everything?"

Alas, the distorted name did not save the professor from subsequent events, which began the very next day, turning Persikov's entire life upside down.

After knocking, Pankrat entered the laboratory and handed Persikov a magnificent satin business card.

"He's over there's," Pankrat added timidly.

The elegant font on the card read:

ALFRED ARKADIEVICH
BRONSKY

Correspondent for the Moscow magazines
Red Flame, *Red Pepper*, *Red Magazine*, *Red Projector*,
and the newspaper *Red Evening News*.

"Throw him the hell out," Persikov said monotonously and brushed the card under the table.

Pankrat turned around and left, only to return five minutes later with a pained expression and a second copy of the same card.

"Is this a joke?" Persikov screeched and became frightening.

"They says they is from the Gee-Pee-Yoo[1]," Pankrat replied, growing pale.

Persikov grabbed the card with one hand, nearly tearing it in half, and threw his tweezers on the table with the other. Curly handwriting on the card read: "Please forgive me and I would appreciate, esteemed professor, three minutes of your time on public press business and as correspondent of the satirical magazine *Red Raven*, a GPU publication."

"Send him in here," Persikov said breathlessly.

A young man with a clean-shaven, oily faced jumped instantly from behind Pankrat's back. He had perpetually raised eyebrows, like a Chinaman, and shifty agate eyes that never looked directly at anyone. The young man was dressed impeccably according to the latest fashion: long, narrow jacket stretching almost to his knees, broad bell-shaped trousers, and unnaturally wide patent leather shoes with their toes resembling hooves. The young man was holding a cane, a pointy hat, and a notebook.

"What do you want," Persikov asked in a voice that made Pankrat disappear immediately behind the door. "Were you not told that I am busy?"

1 *GPU* – Russian acronym for State Political Administration, secret police of the Soviet Union from 1922 until 1934 and predecessor of the KGB.

Instead of responding, the young man bowed twice to the professor, once to the left and once to the right, and then his eyes wheeled over the entire lab, and he immediately made a mark in his notebook.

"I am busy," the professor said, looking into the eyes of the guest with disgust, but this had no effect because the shifty little eyes were impossible to catch.

"A thousand apologies, esteemed sir professor," the young man began in a high-pitched voice, "that I am barging in on you and taking up your precious time, but the news about your amazing discovery, which has shaken the entire world, has forced our magazine to ask you for some sort of explanation."

"What explanations for the entire world?" Persikov whined in a shrill voice, turning yellow. "I have no obligation to give you any sort of explanation, or some such... I am busy... terribly busy."

"What are you working on?" the young man asked sweetly and made a second mark in his notebook.

"I... look, you... you want to print something?"

"Yes," the young man said and suddenly began to scribble rapidly in his notebook.

"Firstly, I have no intention to publish anything until I complete my work... especially not in all those papers of yours... Secondly, how do you know about all this?" Suddenly, Persikov felt lost.

"Is it true that you have invented the ray of new life?"

"What new life?" the professor became furious. "Stop spouting nonsense! The ray I am working on has not been properly investigated, and we do not know anything! There is a possibility that it can raise the activity levels of protoplasm..."

"How many fold?" the young man asked hurriedly.

Persikov felt utterly lost now. "Some character. Hell alone knows what's going on!"

"What's the point of these layman questions? Let's assume, I would say, about a thousand fold!"

A predatory joy flashed in the young man's eyes.

"You can obtain gigantic organisms?"

"Nothing of the sort! Well, it's true that the organisms I have obtained are larger than normal... Well, so they have some new properties... But the main point here is not the size, but the unbelievable speed of reproduction," Persikov said, to his own misfortune, and was immediately horrified by his own words. The young man had already filled up an entire page; he turned it and continued to scribble.

"Stop writing!" Persikov wheezed in despair, giving up and realizing that he was fully in the young man's hands. "What are you writing?"

"Is it true that you can produce two million tadpoles from frog eggs over the course of two days?"

"From how many eggs?" Persikov shouted, furious again. "Have you ever even seen an egg of... oh say, a tree frog?"

"From half a pound of eggs?" the young man asked, unfazed.

Persikov turned purple.

"What sort of measure is that? Bah! What are you talking about? Well, of course, if you were to take half a pound of frog eggs... then perhaps... hell, well maybe around that amount, maybe even much more!"

The young man's eyes lit up like diamonds, and he filled up another page in one fell swoop.

"Is it true that this will cause a worldwide revolution in live-stock-rearing?"

"What a tabloid question!" Persikov howled. "And, at any rate, I give you no permission to print such nonsense. I can see by your face that you are writing something vile!"

"Your photograph, professor, if you would please indulge us," the young man spoke, closing his notebook.

"What? My photograph? In your little magazines? Along with that hellish garbage you print? No, no, no... and I am busy... I have to ask you to leave!"

"At least an old one. We'll return it to you right away."

"Pankrat!" the professor shouted in rage.

"It was a pleasure to meet you," the young man said, disappearing.

Instead of Pankrat, a strange, regular creaking of some mechanism came from behind the door, along with the terse sound of something hammering on the floor, and a man of unusual girth appeared in the laboratory, dressed in a blouse and pants made of blanket wool. His artificial left leg clicked and rumbled, and there was a briefcase in his hands. His round, clean-shaven face, which resembled yellowish jellied meat, displayed a friendly smile. He bowed to the professor in a military fashion and straightened, which caused his leg to emit a spring-like click. Persikov was dumbfounded.

"Sir professor," the stranger began in a pleasant, somewhat hoarse voice. "Please forgive this mere mortal who has disturbed your solitude."

"Are you a reporter?" Persikov asked. "Pankrat!!"

"Not at all, sir professor," the fat man replied. "Please allow me to introduce myself – I am a seafaring captain and contributor at the *Industry Herald* newspaper produced by the Soviet of People's Commissars."

"Pankrat!!" Persikov shouted hysterically, and at that exact moment, the phone in the corner raised a red flag and rang out softly. "Pankrat!" the professor repeated. "I'm listening…"

"Verzeihen Sie bitte, Herr Professor," the phone rasped in German, "dass ich störe. Ich bin Mitarbeiter des 'Berliner Tageblatts'[2]…"

"Pankrat," the professor shouted into the receiver. "Bin momental sehr beschäftigt und kann Sie deshalb jetzt nicht empfangen![3] Pankrat!!"

And then the doorbell began to ring at the main entrance of the institute.

2 (German) Please forgive me for bothering you, sir professor. I am a correspondent of the Berlin Daily.

3 (German) I am busy at the moment and cannot speak to you.

* * *

"Horrific murder on Bronnaya Street!!" wailed unnatu-ral, hoarse voices, whirling around in the thick of lights amid the wheels and flashing headlights on the hot June pavement. "Horrific ailment of chickens belonging to the priest's widow Drozdova, her picture is included! Horrific discovery of the life ray by Professor Persikov!!"

Persikov dashed for it so quickly that he was nearly hit by a car on Mokhovaya and grasped the paper fiercely.

"Three kopeks, mister!" the boy screamed, and, squeezing into the crowd on the sidewalk, began howling again: "*Red Eve-ning News*, the discovery of the X-ray!!"

The dumbfounded Persikov opened the newspaper and pressed against a lamppost. On the left side of the second page, a bald man with a hanging lower jaw and crazed, unsee-ing eyes was staring at him from a smudged frame. It was the fruit of Alfred Bronsky's artistic efforts. "V. I. Persikov, who discovered the mysterious red ray," read the caption beneath the drawing. Below it was an article with the heading "A Global Mystery." It began with:

"'Have a seat,' the venerable scientist Persikov said to us amicably…"

The article was signed by: "Alfred Bronsky (Alonzo)."

A greenish light soared over the roofs of the university, the fiery words "Talking Paper" appeared in the sky, and a crowd flooded Mokhovaya.

"'Have a seat!!!'" a most unpleasant, high-pitched voice howled suddenly from a loudspeaker on the roof, greatly re-sembling the voice of Alfred Bronsky magnified a thousand times, "the venerable scientist Persikov said to us amicably! 'I had long wanted to tell the proletariat of Moscow about my discovery…'"

The quiet mechanical creaking appeared behind Persikov's back, and someone tugged on his sleeve. Turning around,

Persikov saw the round, yellow face of the owner of the mechanical leg. His eyes were watering and his lips trembling.

"You didn't choose to share the results of your amazing
discovery with me, sir professor," he said mournfully and gave
a heavy sigh. "There goes my pittance."

He glanced dejectedly at the roof of the university, where
an unseen Alfred was raving somewhere in the black maw of
the loudspeaker. For some reason, Persikov took pity on the
fat man.

"I never told him to have a seat," he muttered, catching the
words from the sky with hatred. "He is just an incredibly inso-
lent scoundrel! Forgive me, please, but when someone barges
in when you are working... I don't mean you, of course..."

"Perhaps you would at least be willing to describe your
chamber for me, sir professor?" the mechanical man said in-
gratiatingly and mournfully. "It's all the same to you now, after
all..."

"In three days, half a pound of eggs produces so many
tadpoles that there is absolutely no way to count them," the
invisible man roared into the loudspeaker.

"Toot-toot," the cars on Mokhovaya shouted dully.

"Ho-ho-ho... listen to that, ho-ho-ho," the crowd rustled,
looking upwards.

"What a scoundrel! Eh?" Persikov hissed to the mechanical man, trembling in indignation. "How do you like that? I'm
going to file a complaint against him!"

"Outrageous!" the fat man agreed.

A brilliant violet ray blinded the professor, lighting up the
lamppost, a section of the paved roadway, the yellow wall, curious faces.

"That's for you, sir professor," the fat man whispered with
delight, hanging on to the professor's sleeve like a lead weight.
Something rattled in the air.

"Ah, to hell with all of them!" Persikov exclaimed drearily,
tearing out of the crowd along with his lead weight. "Hey, taxi.
To Prechistenka!"

A peeling old 1924 model car warbled near the sidewalk, and the professor began to climb into the back, trying to detach himself from the fat man.

"You are in my way," he hissed, shielding himself from the violet light with his fists.

"Did you read it? What's it say? Professor Persikov was butchered on Malaya Bronnaya along with his kids!!" they shouted in the crowd.

"I don't have any kids, you sons of bitches!" Persikov bellowed and suddenly came into the focus of a black camera that snapped him in profile view, with an open mouth and angry eyes.

"Krrrh... toot... krrrh... toot," the taxi shouted, cutting into the thick of the traffic.

The fat man was already sitting in the seat, warming the professor's side.

Chapter 5

★

The Chicken Story

In a small district town, formerly Troitsky, now known as Steklovsk, Kostroma province, Stekolniy district, a woman wearing a grey dress with chintz flowers and a kerchief tied round her head walked out on the porch of a little house on the former Sobornaya, now Personal Street, and began to weep bitterly. The woman – the widow of Drozdov, former archpriest of a former cathedral – wept so loudly that soon a woman's head in a woolly kerchief emerged from the window of the house across the street and exclaimed:

"What's wrong, Stepanovna, is't more of the same?"

"The seventeenth one!" the former Drozdova replied, drowning in tears.

"Oh-oh-dear," the woman began to whimper, shaking her head. "What's going on already? The Lord is angry, and if that ain't the truth! Gone and died?"

"Just look, look Matryona," the priest's widow muttered with loud, painful sobs. "Look what's got in her!"

The slanting gray gate banged, the woman's bare feet plodded over the dusty humps of the street, and the tear-stained widow led Matryona into the chicken yard.

One should say that the widow of the archpriest, Father Sawaty Drozdov, who passed away in 1926 from anti-religious pains, did not lose heart at all but instead managed to organize a wonderful chicken farm. As soon as the widow's business began to blossom, she was assessed with such enormous taxes that the chicken farm would have gone under were it not for a few nice folk. They told the widow to write a

declaration to the local authorities stating that she was orga-
nizing a workers' poultry cooperative. The cooperative con-
sisted of Drozdova herself, her faithful servant Matryona,
and the widow's deaf niece. The tax was retracted, and by
1928 the chicken farm had become so successful that as many
as two hundred and fifty chickens, including even a few Co-
chins[1], were walking around the widow's dusty yard, girdled
by chicken coops. The widow's eggs appeared every Sunday
on the market at Steklovsk, they were sold in Tambov, and
they even appeared occasionally in the glass windows of the
store formerly known as "Cheechkin's Cheese and Butter in
Moscow."

And so, that morning alone, the seventeenth Brahmaputra[2]
– a beloved crested hen – was walking around the yard and
vomiting. "Er… rr… url… url… ho-ho-ho," the crested hen
pronounced, rolling her sad eyes at the sun as if she were seeing it for the last time. Cooperative member Matryona hopped
in front of her with a cup of water.

"Cresty, darling… chuck-chuck-chuck… have a drink of
water," Matryona pleaded, chasing the crested hen's beak with
the cup, but the hen would have none of it… She would open
wide her beak and throw back her head. Then she would vomit
blood.

"Jesuschrist!" cried the guest, slapping her thighs. "What's
going on here? It's curdling blood. As I'm standing here, I've
never seen a hen sick to the stomach, like a human being."

Those were the parting words for the poor crested hen. She
tumbled suddenly on her side, pecked helplessly at the ground,
and rolled up her eyes. Then she turned on her back, thrust
both legs in the air, and lay still. Matryona began to cry in a
deep voice, spilling the water in the cup, and the priest's widow
– the chairman of the cooperative – began to cry as well. The
guest leaned to her ear and began to whisper:

---

1 *Cochin* – A breed of chicken originating from China.
2 *Brahmaputra* – A breed of chicken originating from the Brahmaputra
region in India.

"Stepanovna, I'll eat dirt if someone hasn't put the evil eye on your chickens. Who's ever seen anything like this? Chickens don't even got diseases like that! Someone's put a spell on your chickens."

"Jealous enemies!" the widow exclaimed to the heavens. "Do they want me done in for good?"

A loud rooster's crow was the response to her words, and then a lean, ragged rooster tore sideways from a chicken coop, like a restless drunk from a pub. He bulged out his eyes savagely at them, stomped around on one spot for a while, spreading his wings like an eagle, only instead of soaring away he began to run around the yard in a circle, like a tethered horse. On his third lap he stopped and threw up, then began to hack and wheeze, spitting out spots of blood, and finally turned over and directed his legs at the sun like masts. Women's howls shook the yard. And anxious clucking, flapping, and fussing came from the chicken coops in response.

"What else if not evil eye?" the guest asked victoriously. "Call Father Sergius, let 'im ward it off."

At six o'clock in the evening, when the fiery snout of the sun was sitting low between the mugs of young sunflowers, Father Sergius, head priest of the cathedral, finished his prayer and took off his stole. The heads of curious onlookers peeked over and through the cracks of the ancient wooden fence. Kissing the cross, the mournful widow amply moistened a torn yellow ruble with her tears and handed it to Father Sergius, who sighed and said something to the effect of the Lord being angry at us, see. Throughout all this, Father Sergius looked like he knew exactly why the Lord was angry, but would not say.

Thereafter, the crowd on the street dissipated, and since chickens go to sleep early, no one discovered that, in the chicken coop belonging to the widow's neighbor, three hens and a rooster had perished at once. They were throwing up just like Drozdova's chickens, only the deaths occurred quietly inside the coop. The rooster tumbled headfirst from the perch and expired in that position. As for the widow's chickens, they kicked the bucket right after the service, and, come evening, the chicken coops were dead and silent, filled with piles of stiffened poultry.

The next morning, the town was thunderstruck, because the story had taken a widespread, monstrous turn. By noon, only three hens remained alive on all of Personal Street, in the house on the very end, rented by the local financial inspector, but even those went belly up by one o'clock. And in the evening, the entire town of Steklovsk was humming and seething like a beehive, and the menacing word "plague" was propagating through it. Drozdova's name appeared in the local paper *Red Soldier*, under the heading: "Could It Be Chicken Plague?" and then the story passed on to Moscow.

* * *

Professor Persikov's life took on a strange, worrisome, and anxious hue. In other words, it was impossible to work under such conditions. One day after he tangled with Alfred Bronsky, he was forced to disable the phone at the institute by removing the receiver from the hook. And that evening, riding the streetcar along Hunter's Row, the professor saw his own image on the roof of an enormous building bearing the sign "WORKERS' PAPER" in black letters. Flickering and blinking in greenish color, he, the professor, was climbing into the back seat of a taxi with the round mechanical man dressed in blanket wool holding on to his sleeve. On the white screen on the roof, the professor was shielding himself with his fists from the violet ray. Then a fiery inscription appeared: "Traveling by car, Professor Persikov explains his work to our famous reporter Captain Stepanov." And indeed: there was the hazy image of an automobile zooming along Volkhonka, past the Church of Christ the Savior, with the professor bouncing around in it, looking a cornered wolf.

"They are devils, not people," the zoologist muttered through his teeth as he passed by.

On the evening of the same day, upon returning to his place on Prechistenka, the zoologist received seventeen notes from the housekeeper Maria Stepanovna with the phone numbers of those who had called him while he was away. He also received the verbal statement from Maria Stepanovna that she was exhausted. The professor wanted to tear up the notes but then stopped short because he saw the words "People's Commissar of Health" next to one of the numbers.

"What is going on?" thought the learned crank, genuinely perplexed. "What's gotten into them?"

The doorbell rang at a quarter past ten on the same evening, and the professor was forced to talk to some dazzlingly dressed gentleman. The professor agreed to see him because of his business card, which said (without a name or surname): "Authorized head of foreign trade department representatives in the Soviet Republic."

"To hell with him," Persikov growled, tossing a magnifying glass and some diagrams down on the green fabric of the desk, and said to Maria Stepanovna: "Bring him here to the study, that authorized what's his face."

"How may I be of service?" Persikov asked in a tone of voice that made the authorized head flinch. Persikov moved his glasses from the bridge of his nose to his forehead, then back again, and examined the visitor. The latter was glowing with patent leather and precious stones, and a monocle sat in his right eye. "What a filthy snout," Persikov thought for some reason.

The guest began in a roundabout way by asking for permission to light a cigar, after which Persikov invited him very reluctantly to sit down. Then the guest apologized at length for having come so late: "But... it is so difficult to catch... hee-hee, I beg pardon... to find the esteemed professor at home during the day" (the guest sniveled like a hyena when he laughed).

"Yes, I am busy!" Persikov replied so curtly that the guest flinched a second time.

Nevertheless, he allowed himself to trouble the famous scientist... time is money, as they say... does the cigar bother the professor?

"Hrrm-hrrm-hrrm," Persikov replied. And so, he allowed himself to trouble...

"The professor has discovered the ray of life, has he not?"

"Please, what ray of life? It's an invention of the newspapers!" Persikov livened up.

"Oh, no, hee-hee-heh." He understands perfectly well the modesty that truly distinguishes a real scientist... but of course... Telegrams have been sent today... In the various cities of the world, such as Warsaw and Riga, everyone knows about the ray. The entire world is repeating the name of Professor Persikov... The entire world is watching Professor Persikov's work with bated breath... But everyone knows how hard it is for scientists in Soviet Russia. *Entre nous soit dit*...[3] Are we alone in here? Alas, they do not value scientific work in this country, and so he would like to discuss something with the professor... A certain foreign state would like to offer completely selfless assistance to Professor Persikov in his work. Why cast pearls, as the holy book says? This foreign state knows how difficult the professor's life had been in 1919 and 1920 during this whole, hee-hee... revolution. Now, this would be completely secret, of course... the professor will acquaint the foreign state with the results of his work, and in return it will sponsor the professor. For example, the professor has built a chamber – it would be interesting to take a look at the blueprints of this chamber...

And then the guest took a pristine wad of bills out of his inside pocket...

For example, the professor can receive this mere trifle, five thousand rubles, as an advance, right this minute... And there's no need for a receipt... The professor will even hurt the feelings of the authorized head of trade if he brings up a receipt.

---

3 (French) Between us.

"Out!!!" Persikov barked so horribly all of a sudden that the piano in the living room emitted a high-pitched noise.

The guest disappeared so quickly that Persikov, still shaking with rage a minute later, had begun to doubt whether the whole thing had been real or a hallucination.

"Are these his galoshes?" Persikov howled shortly thereafter from the front hall.

"He forgot them," a trembling Maria Stepanovna replied.

"Throw them out!"

"How can I throw them out? He'll come back for them."

"Take them to the building committee. Get a receipt. Don't let me ever see them again! To the committee! Let them take the spy's galoshes!"

Crossing herself, Maria Stepanovna took the fabulous galoshes and carried them out the back door. Then she stood behind the door for a bit and hid the galoshes in the closet.

"Did you do it?" Persikov stormed.

"I did."

"Give me the receipt."

"But, Vladimir Ipatievich, the chairman is illiterate!"

"Get. A. Receipt. Right. This. Second. Find some literate son of a bitch and get him to sign!"

Maria Stepanovna shook her head, departed, and came back a quarter hour later with a note:

"Received from Prof. Persikov, 1 (one) pr galo. Signed, Kolesov."

"And what's this?"

"The claim tag."

Persikov trampled the tag on the floor and put the note under a paperweight. Then a certain thought clouded his steep forehead. He dashed to the phone, dialed Pankrat at the institute, and asked him: "Is everything all right?" Pankrat growled something into the receiver that suggested that, in his opinion, everything was all right. But Persikov only calmed down for a short while. Frowning, he grasped the phone and said this into the receiver:

"Get me, what's her face... Lubyanka[4]. *Merci*... Listen, one of you needs to know... I have suspicious characters in galoshes traipsing through my apartment, yes... Professor Persikov from Fourth University..."

The receiver interrupted the conversation very abruptly. Persikov stepped away from the phone, grumbling obscenities through his teeth.

"Will you be having tea, Vladimir Ipatievich," Maria Stepanovna inquired timidly, glancing into the study.

"I don't want any tea... hrrm-hrrm-hrrm, and to hell with all of them... it's like something bit them."

Exactly ten minutes later, the professor was seeing new visitors in his study. One of them – a pleasant, round, very polite gentleman – was wearing a modest khaki military coat and breeches. A pince-nez sat on his nose, resembling a crystal butterfly. He resembled an angel in patent leather boots. The second man was very short, awfully gloomy, and although he wore civilian clothes, they seemed to make him uncomfortable. The third guest acted differently from the first two; he did not go into the study, but remained in the dimly lit front hall. Nevertheless, he could see the entire study, which was brightly lit and threaded with wisps of tobacco smoke. A smoky pince-nez decorated the face of this third character, who was also wearing civilian clothes.

The two men in the study drove Persikov to utter exhaustion as they examined the business card, asked about the five thousand rubles, and made him describe the appearance of his guest.

"Hell knows," Persikov mumbled. "Repulsive mug. A real degenerate."

"Did he have a glass eye?" the short man asked hoarsely.

"Hell knows. No, wait, it wasn't glass – his eyes were darting."

"Rubinstein?" the angel asked the short plainclothes man. But the latter shook his head grimly.

4 *Lubyanka* – Refers to the headquarters of the Soviet secret police in Lubyanka Square in Moscow.

"Rubinstein would not give him the money without a receipt, never," he grumbled. "This isn't Rubinstein's work. This is someone bigger."

The incident with the galoshes caused a burst of excitement among the guests. The angel said several words on the phone to the building committee: "The State Political Administration needs the building committee secretary Kolesov to report to Professor Persikov's apartment with the galoshes." And immediately, a pale Kolesov appeared in the study, holding the galoshes in his hands.

"Vasenka!" the angel called out quietly to the man sitting in the front hall. The man got up lazily and trudged, as if broken, into the study. The smoky lenses of his pince-nez swallowed his eyes completely.

"Well?" he said laconically in a sleepy voice.

"The galoshes."

The smoky eyes slid over the galoshes, and it seemed to Persikov that, for a brief moment, a pair of extremely sharp and not at all sleepy eyes had flashed sideways beneath the lenses. But the eyes faded immediately.

"Well, Vasenka?"

The one called Vasenka answered in a weary voice:

"Well, what about it? These are Pelenzhkovsky's galoshes."

The building committee was immediately deprived of Professor Persikov's gift. The galoshes disappeared in a newspaper wrapper. Extremely pleased, the angel in the military coat got up and shook the professor's hand, even pronouncing a short speech that could be summarized as follows: this incident does honor to the professor... the professor may rest easy... no one is going to bother him anymore, either at home or at the institute... they will take measures, and his chambers are completely safe...

"Could you possibly have the reporters shot?" Persikov asked, looking over his glasses.

This question amused the guests considerably. Not only the gloomy short man, but even the smoky man in the front hall smiled. Sparkling and shining, the angel explained that it was not possible.

"And who was the scoundrel that was here?"

Here they stopped smiling, and the angel replied evasively that it was nothing, some small-time opportunist, and to pay no mind... but nevertheless he was requesting that the professor maintain strict secrecy about the events of this evening. And the guests departed.

Persikov returned to his study and to the diagrams, but he was not fated to get any work done. An orange light appeared on the phone, and a woman's voice asked the professor if he was interested in marrying a fascinating and passionate widow with a seven-room apartment. Persikov howled into the receiver:

"You should go and get your head checked by Professor Rossolimo..." and then he received a second call.

Here Persikov went somewhat limp because a rather well-known figure was calling from the Kremlin in order to question him sympathetically and at length about his work, and express the desire to visit his laboratory. Stepping away from the phone, Persikov wiped his forehead and left the receiver off the hook. Then the horrible sound of brass instruments and the howling of Valkyries came from the apartment upstairs – the radio belonging to the director of the fabric trust had picked up Wagner's concert being broadcast from the Bolshoi Theater. To the howling and thundering coming from the ceiling, Persikov announced to Maria Stepanovna that he would take the director to court, that he would break his radio, that he would get the hell out of Moscow, because evidently someone was trying to drive him out. He broke his magnifying glass and fell asleep on the couch in the study to the tender key fingering of a famous pianist coming from the Bolshoi Theater.

The next day, the surprises continued. Upon arriving at the institute by streetcar, Persikov found an unknown gentleman in a fashionable green bowler hat standing on the porch. The gentleman scrutinized Persikov but did not pester him with questions, so Persikov tolerated his presence. But in the front hall of the institute, a second bowler hat rose to greet Persikov along with a confused Pankrat:

"Hello, mister professor."

"What do you want?" Persikov asked in a terrifying voice, tearing off his coat with Pankrat's assistance. But the bowler calmed Persikov down right away, whispering in a most tender voice that the professor's concern was unwarranted. He, the bowler, was here for the express purpose of ridding the professor of various annoying visitors... the professor could rest easy not only about the doors of his laboratory, but also the windows. Then the unknown man turned over the lapel of his jacket for an instant and flashed some kind of badge at the professor.

"Hmm... you people really know your business," Persikov mumbled and then asked naively: "But what are you going to eat around here?"

The bowler smirked and explained that someone would come to relieve him.

The next three days went very well. Persikov only had two visitors from the Kremlin, and the students came once for their exam. All the students failed, and their faces showed that Persikov now filled them with a truly superstitious fear.

"Go be streetcar conductors! You are not fit to study zoology," came from the laboratory.

"Strict?" the bowler asked Pankrat.

"God forbid you run afoul of him," Pankrat replied. "If one ever makes it to the end of the exam, poor soul comes out of the laboratory swaying and sweating like a pig. And then straight to the pub."

With all these concerns, the professor barely noticed three days pass, but on the fourth day, he was once again exposed to the outside world, and the cause of this was a shrill, high-pitched voice from the street.

"Vladimir Ipatievich!" the voice shouted from Herzen Street into the open window of the laboratory. The voice got lucky: the last three days had left Persikov too drained. At that moment, he was resting in his chair, smoking and staring weakly and vacantly into space with red-rimmed eyes. He could not take it anymore. And as a result he peeked out the window with almost a measure of curiosity and saw Alfred Bronsky on the sidewalk. The professor recognized the multi-titled owner of the satin business card right away by his pointy hat and his notebook. Bronsky bowed gently and respectfully at the window.

"Oh, it's you?" asked the professor. He was too tired to be angry, and he was even slightly curious as to what would happen next. Protected by the window, he felt safe from Alfred. The ever-present bowler on the street turned his head immediately towards Bronsky. A very sweet smile blossomed on Bronsky's face.

"Just one-two minutes, my dear professor," Bronsky began from the sidewalk, straining his voice. "Just one question, and purely a zoological one. Permit me to ask?"

"Ask," Persikov replied laconically with a degree of irony and thought: "There really is something American about this bastard."

"What do you have to say as for the chickens, my dear professor?" Bronsky shouted, cupping his hands.

Persikov was astounded. He sat down on the windowsill, then got up, pushed a button, and shouted, pointing his finger at the window:

"Pankrat, let him in, from the sidewalk."

When Bronsky appeared in the laboratory, Persikov extended his courtesy so much that be barked:

"Have a seat!"

Smiling rapturously, Bronsky sat down on a revolving stool.

"Tell me, please," Persikov began, "do you write for all those papers of yours?"

"Yes sir," Alfred answered respectfully.

"And so, I don't understand how you can write when you cannot even speak properly. What are all these 'one-two minutes' and 'as for the chickens?' You probably meant 'about the chickens?'"

Bronsky emitted a thin, respectful laugh.

"Valentin Petrovich edits it."

"Who is Valentin Petrovich?"

"Head of the literary department."

"Very well. I'm not a philologist anyway. Leave aside your Petrovich. What is it you wish to know about chickens?"

"Anything you care to say, professor."

Bronsky armed himself with a pencil. Victorious sparks appeared in Persikov's eyes.

"You really should not have come to me, I do not specialize in fowl. You should try Yemelian Ivanovich Portugalov, from First University. Myself, I know very little…"

Bronsky smiled rapturously, showing that he understood the dear professor's joke. "Joke – knows little!" he scribbled in his notebook.

"However, since you asked, here you are. Chickens, or jungle-fowl… are a genus of fowl from the order of *Galliformes*. From the pheasant family…" Persikov began in a loud voice, looking not at Bronsky but somewhere into the distance, the presumed location of an audience of thousands. "From the pheasant family… *Phaisanidae*. They are birds with a fleshy skin crest and two hanging processes beneath their lower jaw… hmm… although occasionally there is only one in the middle of the chin… What else? The wings are short and rounded… The tail is of average length, somewhat staggered, I would even say roof-shaped, the middle feathers form a sickle-like curve… Pankrat, bring me model no. 705 from the model cases, cross-section of a rooster… Then again, you don't need it, do you? Pankrat, do not bring the model… I repeat, I am not a specialist, try Portugalov. Now, I personally know six species of wild chickens… Hmm… Portugalov knows more… In India and the Malayan archipelago… For example, the Bankiva rooster, or Kazinthu, is found in the foothills of the Himalayas, throughout India, in Assam, in Burma… the swallow-tailed rooster, or *Gallus varius*, is found on

Lombok, Sumbawa, and Flores. And on the island of Java, you can find the remarkable rooster *Gallus aeneus*, while in southeast India I recommend the very beautiful *sonneratii* rooster... I'll show you a picture later. Now, as for Ceylon, here we meet the Stanley rooster, which is not found anywhere else."

Bronsky sat with his eyes bulging out and scribbled in his notebook.

"Would you care to hear anything else?"

"I would like to find out about chicken ailments," Alfred whispered very quietly.

"Hmm, well I'm no specialist... ask Portugalov... Then again... Well, there are tapeworms, flukes, scabies mites, red mange, bird mites, chicken lice, fleas, chicken cholera, croupous-diptheric inflammation of the mucous membranes... Pneumoconiosis, tuberculosis, chicken mange... who knows what else..." (sparks were flashing in Persikov's eyes) "poisoning – by henbane, for example – tumors, rickets, jaundice, rheumatism, the fungus *Achorion schoenleinii*... a very interesting ailment: the symptoms involve little spots on the crest, resembling mold..."

Bronsky wiped the sweat from his brow with a handkerchief.

"And, in your opinion, professor, what is the cause of the current catastrophe?"

"What catastrophe?"

"You haven't read about it, professor?" Bronsky said in surprise and extracted a wrinkled sheet of *Izvestiya* from his briefcase.

"I don't read newspapers," Persikov replied, frowning.

"But why not, professor?" Alfred asked tenderly.

"Because they print nonsense," Persikov replied without hesitation.

"But professor..." Bronsky whispered softly and unfolded the sheet.

"What's this?" Persikov asked and even got up from his seat.

Now the sparks were dancing in Bronsky's eyes. With his sharp, manicured finger he underscored an incredibly huge headline running the entire width of the paper: "CHICKEN PLAGUE IN THE REPUBLIC."

"What?" Persikov said, moving his glasses to his forehead...

CHAPTER 6

★

MOSCOW IN JUNE OF 1928

It glowed; the lights were dancing, fading, and flashing. The white headlights of buses and green streetcar lamps whirled around Theater Square. Over the former Muir & Mirrielees, on top of the newly added tenth floor, a multicolored electrical woman jumped around, tossing out multicolored words letter by letter: "WORKERS' CREDIT." A crowd pushed and hummed in the small park across from the Bolshoi Theater, near a fountain illuminated by multicolored lights at night. And over the Bolshoi Theater itself, a giant loudspeaker was howling:

"The chicken vaccines developed at the Lefortovo Veterinary Institute have produced dazzling results. The number of chicken deaths dropped in half today."

Then the loudspeaker changed its tone; something roared inside it, a green spray flashed and faded out over the theater, and the loudspeaker began to complain in a deep voice:

"A special committee has been formed to combat the chicken plague, consisting of the People's Commissar of Health, the People's Commissar of Agriculture, the head of the livestock-rearing department – comrade Birdov-Porcinsky, Professors Persikov and Portugalov... and comrade Rabinovich! New attempts at interventionism[1]," the loudspeaker laughed and howled like a jackal, "linked to the chicken plague!"

Theatre Drive, Neglinny, and Lubyanka were ablaze with white and violet stripes, splashing rays of light, full of howling

1 Foreign interventionism and spying, both substantiated and unsubstantiated, played an important role in Soviet propaganda.

car horns and clouds of dust floating in the air. Crowds of people had amassed by the walls plastered with large notices, lit by harsh red reflectors:

> "The consumption of chicken meat and eggs is forbidden to the public and will be punished to the full extent of the law. Private merchants attempting to sell these commodities in marketplaces will be subject to criminal prosecution and confiscation of all personal property. All citizens in possession of eggs must immediately surrender them to local police stations."

On the screen over the roof of *Workers' Paper*, piles of chickens towered into the sky, and green-tinted firemen, fragmenting and sparkling, were hosing them with kerosene. Then waves of red passed over the screen, an unnatural smoke welled up, floating in shreds and creeping in streams, and a fiery caption appeared: "Burning of dead chickens on Hodynka."

Among the furiously shining storefronts, open until 3am with two breaks for lunch and dinner, boarded-up windows were staring blindly at the street beneath signs that read: "Eggs for sale. Quality guaranteed." Hissing cars would speed frequently past the policemen, wailing anxiously, with inscriptions on the sides: "MosHealthDept Ambulance."

"Another one stuffing his face with rotten eggs," the crowd would rustle.

The world-famous Empire Restaurant flashed its green and orange lights on the Petrovsky Lines, and inside, on the small tables by the portable phones, were liqueur-stained cardboard signs: "By MosSoviet regulation, omelets are not available. Fresh oysters have been delivered."

At the Hermitage, where small Chinese lamps shone like pitiful beads amid the dead, stifled greenery, on a stage flooded with piercing light that blinded the eyes, the singers Shramms and Karmanchikov were performing ditties composed by the poets Ardo and Arguyev:

> "Oh mama, what am I to do
> Without my eggs?"

…and tap-dancing thunderously.

The theater named in honor of the late Vsevolod Mejerhold – who, as you know, died in 1927 during a production of Pushkin's "Boris Godunov," when the trapezes with the naked boyars[2] collapsed on him – flung out a multi-colored, moving electrical sign announcing a play by the dramatist Erendorf called "Chicken Doom," directed by Mejerhold's student, the distinguished Director of the Republic Kukhterman. Next door, at the Aquarium, to the sparkling of neon advertisements and the flashing of half-naked women's bodies, the revue "Sons of Chickens" by the writer Lenivtsev was staged to thunderous applause amid the greenery of the stage. And on Tverskaya, circus donkeys walked in rows, with lights hung on either side of their heads, bearing shining posters: "Rostand's 'Chantecler' is on again at the Korsh Theater."

The paper boys growled and howled amid the wheels of the cars:

"Horrific discovery in an underground cave! Poland bracing for horrific war! Professor Persikov's horrific experiments!!!"

In the former Nikitin's Circus, on a greasy brown arena that smelled pleasantly of manure, the deathly-pale clown Bom was telling the clown Bim, who was swollen with checkered dropsy:

"I know why you are so sad!"

"Vai?" Bim asked in a squeaking voice.

"You buried your eggs in the yard, and the police from the 15th precinct found them."

---

2 *Boyar* – The highest-ranking member of Russian feudal aristocracy.

"Ha-ha-ha-ha," the circus erupted in laughter, chilling the blood with happiness and longing as trapezes and cobwebs floated beneath the ancient dome.

"Ah-hup!" the clowns shouted piercingly, and a well-fed white horse brought out a woman of wondrous beauty with slender legs, wearing a crimson leotard.

* * *

Looking at no one, seeing no one, unresponsive to the prodding and the quiet, tender invitations of the prostitutes, the inspired and lonely Persikov, crowned with unexpected fame, was making his way along Mokhovaya towards the burning clock by the Manege. Here, consumed by his own thoughts and not looking where he was going, he bumped into a strange, old-fashioned man and banged his fingers very painfully against the wooden holster hanging on the man's belt.

"Ah, hell!" Persikov squeaked. "Excuse me."

"Pardon me," the passerby replied in an unpleasant voice, and then they somehow managed to disentangle amid the human mass. And the professor headed towards Prechistenka, immediately forgetting the encounter.

Chapter 7

★

Phate

It is unclear whether the Lefortovo veterinary vaccines were particularly effective, whether the quarantine detachments in Samara were particularly skilled, whether the tough measures against egg resellers in Kaluga and Voronezh were particularly helpful, or whether the work of the special commission in Moscow was particularly successful. But it is well known that, two weeks after the last meeting of Persikov and Alfred, the Soviet Union was completely clean and empty, chicken-wise. Orphaned chicken feathers lay in the yards of provincial houses, bringing tears to a few eyes, and the last of the gluttonous were still in the hospitals, recovering from bloody diarrhea and vomiting. Fortunately, no more than a thousand people had died in the entire republic. The civil disturbances were also minimal. True, a prophet had appeared in Volokolamsk and declared that the chicken plague had been caused by none other than the commissars, but he was met with little enthusiasm. Several policemen were beaten up in the Volokolamsk market as they tried to confiscate chickens from the women, and someone smashed the windows in the local post and telegraph office. Fortunately, the prompt Volokolamsk authorities took several measures that resulted in, firstly, the prophet ceasing his activities, and, secondly, the telegraph windows being replaced.

Upon reaching Archangelsk and Siumkin Village in the north, the plague ended all by itself because it had nowhere else to go – as you know, there are no chickens in the White Sea. It also stopped in Vladivostok, for beyond that city lay the ocean. Far in the south, it faded and disappeared somewhere in the scorched expanses of Ordubat, Dzhulfa, and Karabulak, and in the west it stopped miraculously right at the Polish and Romanian borders. Either the climate was slightly different there, or perhaps the quarantine measures taken by the neighboring governments had played a part, but the fact is that the plague did not go further. The foreign press seized greedily and noisily upon the historically unprecedented plague, while the government of the Soviet republics worked quietly and without respite. The special commission to combat the chicken plague was renamed into a special commission to stimulate and rebuild the poultry industry, and was joined by a new special triumvirate consisting of sixteen comrades. "Volunteer-Fowl" was founded, and Persikov and Portugalov were appointed honorary chairmen. Headlines appeared beneath their photographs in the papers: "Massive purchases of foreign eggs" and "Mr. Hughes[1] wants to sabotage the egg campaign." A vitriolic satire by the journalist Kolechkin made a big splash in Moscow; it ended with the words: "Don't covet our eggs, Mr. Hughes – you've got your own!"

The last three weeks had left Professor Persikov completely exhausted and overworked. The chicken events disturbed his routine and burdened him with a double load. He had to spend entire evenings in the chicken commission meetings and occasionally tolerate lengthy conversations with either Alfred Bronsky or the fat mechanical man. Along with Professor Portugalov and private docents Ivanov and Bornhart, he had to dissect and microscope chickens in search of the plague bacillus, and he even spent three evenings hastily penning a brochure entitled: "On changes in the liver of fowl stricken by the plague."

Persikov worked in the fowl field without particular enthusiasm, which was understandable. His entire head was preoccupied with something else – that main, important thing from

1 Charles Evan Hughes Sr. served as the United States Secretary of State from 1921 until 1925.

which he had been distracted by the chicken catastrophe – i.e. the red ray. Upsetting his already strained health and stealing precious hours from food and sleep, sometimes without returning to Prechistenka and sleeping on the oilcloth couch in the institute laboratory, Persikov spent his nights with the chamber and the microscope.

By the end of July, the crunch had eased somewhat. The renamed commission had established a regular routine, and Persikov returned to his interrupted work. The microscopes were loaded with fresh samples, while fish and frog eggs ripened with magical speed in the ray inside the chamber. Specially ordered lenses were delivered by airplane from Konigsberg, and, at the end of July, mechanics supervised by Ivanov constructed two large new chambers, where the ray started off as wide as a pack of cigarettes and expanded to a good meter at the other end. Persikov rubbed his hands together happily and began to prepare for very complex and mysterious experiments. Firstly, he arranged something over the phone with the People's Commissar of Education, and the receiver croaked back pleasantly, promising all sorts of assistance. Then Persikov telephoned comrade Birdov-Porcinsky, head of the livestock-rearing department at the Supreme Commission. Birdov gave Persikov his warmest attention. The matter concerned a large foreign order for Professor Persikov. Birdov said into the phone that he would immediately send telegrams to Berlin and New York. Then the Kremlin called to inquire about Persikov's work, and a dignified, tender voice asked whether Persikov needed a car.

"No, thank you. I prefer to travel by streetcar," Persikov replied.

"But why?" the mysterious voice asked, chuckling condescendingly.

In general, everyone addressed Persikov either with respect and trepidation or with an affectionate chuckle, as if speaking to a young, though important, child.

"It's faster," Persikov replied, after which the sonorous bass in the phone replied:

"Very well, as you wish."

Another week passed by, with Persikov drifting further and further away from the diminishing chicken problems and immersing himself fully into the study of the ray. His head felt light from sleepless nights and exhaustion, as if it had become weightless and transparent. The red circles never left his eyes now, and Persikov spent almost every night at the institute. Once, he abandoned the zoological sanctuary to deliver a lecture about his ray and its effect on egg cells in the gigantic CeCILS[2] Hall on Prechistenka. It was an enormous triumph for the eccentric zoologist. The applause in the colonnaded hall was so loud it practically made the ceiling crumble, and hissing arc lamps poured light onto the black dinner jackets of the CeCILS members and the white dresses of the women. On the stage, next to the podium, a moist, gray-tinted frog the size of a cat was breathing heavily on a glass table. Notes were tossed onto the stage. They included seven love letters, which Persikov later tore up. The president of the commission had to drag him back on stage by force to take a bow. Persikov bowed irritably, his hands were sweaty and moist, and his black tie was somewhere beyond his left ear instead of beneath his chin. In the foggy breathing of the crowd were hundreds of yellowish faces and men's white shirtfronts, and suddenly a yellow pistol holster flashed somewhere and disappeared behind a white column. Persikov noticed it hazily and then forgot about it. But as he departed from the lecture, descending the crimson carpet on the staircase, he suddenly felt unwell. The bright chandelier in the vestibule turned black for an instant, and Persikov felt dizzy, nauseous… He thought he smelled burning, he felt hot, sticky blood pouring down his neck… And the professor grasped the banister with a shaking hand.

2 Central Committee for Improving the Life of Scientists, created in 1921.

"Are you all right, Vladimir Ipatievich?" worried voices came from all directions.

"Yes, yes," Persikov said, recovering. "I am just over-worked... yes... Please, a glass of water."

* * *

It was a very sunny August day. It interfered with the professor's work, so the blinds were down. A single reflector on a flexible leg projected a sharp ray of light onto a glass table littered with tools and lenses. Leaning back in his revolving chair, an exhausted Persikov was smoking a cigarette and staring with dead-tired but satisfied eyes into the slightly open door of the chamber, where the red sheaf of the ray lay quietly, heating the already stuffy and tainted air in the laboratory ever so slightly.

Someone knocked on the door.

"Well?" Persikov asked.

The door creaked softly, and Pankrat came in. Arms at his sides, pale with fear at the sight of the deity, he said the following:

"Phate's come for you, sir professor."

A semblance of smile appeared on the scientist's face. He narrowed his eyes and said:

"That's interesting. Only I'm busy."

"They says they's got an official paper from the Kremlin."

"Fate with a paper? A rare combination," Persikov spoke and then added: "Well, then, let's have a look!"

"Yessir," Pankrat replied and disappeared swiftly behind the door.

A minute later, the door creaked again, and a man appeared on the doorstep. Persikov made a squeaking noise with his chair and stared at the visitor over his shoulder and over his glasses. Persikov was far detached from life, it did not interest him, but even he managed to notice the basic and dominant feature of the man who had entered. He was extremely old-fashioned. In 1919, this man would have fit in perfectly well on the streets of the capital, he would have been tolerated in 1924, or at least in the beginning of that year, but in 1928, he looked very strange. At a time when even the most backward part of the proletariat – the bakers – wore jackets, at a time when military coats were a rarity in Moscow, old-fashioned dress left firmly in 1924, the visitor wore a double-breasted leather jacket, green pants, leggings, and half-boots, while on his side was an enormous old model Mauser pistol in a battered yellow holster. The visitor's face had the same effect on Persikov as it did on everyone else, and this effect was extremely unpleasant. The visitor's tiny eyes stared at the world in surprise and at the same time with over-confidence. There was something unceremonious about his short, flat-footed legs. His face was shaven to a blue sheen. Persikov began to frown right away. The chair croaked merci-lessly, and, now staring at the visitor through his glasses instead of over them, Persikov spoke:

"You have a paper? Where is it?"

The visitor was evidently dumbfounded by what he saw. He rarely found himself at a loss, but now he was. Judging by his little eyes, the initial cause of his shock was the twelve-shelf bookcase towering to the ceiling and packed full of books. Then, of course, there were the chambers, where, swollen up by the lenses, the crimson ray glimmered inside like in hell. And Persikov himself, sitting in his revolving chair in the darkness, near the sharp, needle-like ray emitted by the reflector, was also quite strange and majestic. The visitor directed a stare at him which clearly showed sparks of respect peeking through over-confidence. He did not produce any paper, but instead said:

"I am Alexander Semyonovich Phate!"

"Well? What of it?"

"I am the manager of the Red Ray model state farm[3]," the visitor clarified.

"And?"

"And I'm here to see you, comrade, on secret business."

3 Soviet state-owned farms, or *sovkhozes*, were first created in the 1920s as ideological examples of socialist agriculture.

"I would love to hear all about it. Briefly, if possible."

The visitor opened the flap of his jacket and produced an order printed on excellent thick paper. He handed it to Persikov. And then he sat down on a revolving stool without an invitation.

"Don't push the table," Persikov said hatefully.

The visitor glanced fearfully at the table, where a pair of eyes glimmered lifelessly, like emeralds, in a damp, dark opening at the far end. A coldness emanated from them.

As soon as Persikov read the paper, he got up from his chair and dashed to the phone. In a few seconds, he was already speaking in a hurried and extremely irritated voice:

"Excuse me... I cannot understand... How can it be? I... without my consent, my counsel... Who the hell knows what he'll do?"

Here the stranger turned on the stool, offended.

"Excuse me," he began, "I am the mana..."

But Persikov waved him away with his crooked finger and continued:

"Forgive me, I cannot understand... In the end, I must categorically protest. I will not sanction any experiments with eggs... Not until I try them myself..."

Something tapped and croaked in the receiver, and even from a distance it was possible to see that the condescending voice in the receiver was addressing a small child. The conversation ended with a purple Persikov slamming down the receiver with a thunderous noise and speaking to the wall:

"I wash my hands of this."

He returned to the table, picked up the paper, read it again from top to bottom over his glasses, then from bottom to top through his glasses, and suddenly howled:

"Pankrat!"

Pankrat appeared in the doorway as if he had just emerged from a trap door in an opera. Persikov glanced at him and barked:

"Get out, Pankrat!"

And, without a trace of surprise on his face, Pankrat disappeared.

Then Persikov turned to the visitor and said:

"If you please… I obey. Not my business. And, frankly, I don't care."

The visitor was more amazed than offended at the professor's words.

"I beg pardon," he began, "you, comrade…"

"What's with all your 'comrades…'" Persikov mumbled sullenly.

"Well, now!" said the expression on Phate's face.

"I beg par…"

"Anyway, if you will," Persikov interrupted. "Here is the arc lamp. By moving the eyepiece, you can obtain a ray of light," – Persikov clicked the lid of the chamber, which resembled a camera – "that you can then collect using objectives N1… and the mirror N2," – Persikov extinguished, then relit the ray on the floor of the asbestos chamber – "while you place whatever you want on the floor of the chamber floor and conduct experiments. Extremely simple, is it not?"

Persikov wanted to convey sarcasm and contempt, but the visitor did not notice it as he peered into the chamber carefully with his sparkling little eyes.

"Only, I should warn you," Persikov continued, "that you should not stick your hands into the ray, because, according to my observations, it promotes epithelial growths… and, unfortunately, I have not yet established whether they are malignant or not."

Dropping his leather cap, the visitor hid his hands deftly behind his back and looked at the professor's hands. They were all dark with iodine, and the right one was bandaged near the wrist.

"What about you, professor?"

"You can buy rubber gloves at Schwabe's on Kuznetsky," the professor replied irritably. "This is not my responsibility."

Here Persikov stared at the visitor, as if through a magnifying glass.

"Where did you come from? Anyway... Why you?"

Phate finally took strong offense.

"I beg par..."

"One has to know what he's doing, after all! Why have you latched on to this ray?"

"Because it's a matter of the utmost importance..."

"Uh-huh. The utmost? In that case... Pankrat!"

And when Pankrat appeared:

"Hold on, Pankrat, let me think."

And Pankrat vanished obediently.

"Here is what I cannot understand," Persikov said. "Why all the rush and the secrecy?"

"You've got me all confused, professor," Phate replied. "Surely you know that all the chickens are dead to the very last one."

"So what?" Persikov squealed. "Do you intend to resurrect them instantaneously, then? And why do you want to use a ray that has not been properly studied?"

"Comrade professor," Phate replied, "you are confusing me, honestly. I am telling you that we need to reestablish the poultry industry because they are writing all sorts of filth about us abroad. That's right."

"So let them write..."

"Now, look," Phate replied mysteriously, shaking his head.

"Who came up with the idea of growing chickens from eggs, if I might ask?"

"I did," Phate replied.

"Mm-hmm. Right. And why, if I might ask? How did you find out about the properties of the ray?"

"I was at your lecture, professor."

"I haven't experimented with eggs yet! I was going to!"

"By God, it'll work," Phate said abruptly with conviction and intimacy. "Your ray is so famous it could probably grow elephants, not just chickens."

"You know..." Persikov said, "You are not a zoologist, are you? It's a pity. You would have made a bold experimenter.

Yes… only you risk… failure… and you are wasting my time…"

"We'll return your chambers. What do you mean?"

"When?"

"As soon as I breed the first batch."

"How confidently you say this! Very well. Pankrat!"

"I have people with me," Phate said. "And guards…"

By evening, Persikov's laboratory had become deserted and desolate. The tables were empty. Phate's men had taken the three large chambers, leaving only the first, small one that the professor had used for his first experiments.

July twilight loomed, and grayness took hold of the institute, flowing through the hallways. Monotonous footsteps came from the laboratory – without turning on the lights, Persikov was pacing through the large room from the window to the doors… A strange thing: that evening, an inexplicable melancholy took hold of the people and animals that inhabited the institute. The toads raised a particularly sad chorus, chirping in sinister, forewarning voices. Pankrat had to chase down a grass snake that had escaped from its enclosure, and when he caught it, the snake looked like it wanted nothing more than to leave and never look back.

In the deep dusk, the bell rang in Persikov's laboratory. Pankrat appeared on the doorstep. And there he saw a strange picture. The scientist was standing forlornly in the middle of the laboratory and staring at the tables. Pankrat coughed and froze in place.

"There, Pankrat," Persikov said, pointing at the empty table.

Pankrat was horrified. In the twilight, the professor's eyes looked tear-stained. It was so unnatural, so frightening.

"Yessir," Pankrat replied in a whining voice and thought: "I'd rather you yelled at me or something!"

"There," Persikov repeated, and his lips trembled much like those of a child whose favorite toy had been taken away for no reason.

"You know, my dear Pankrat," Persikov continued, turning towards the window. "My wife, who left fifteen years ago, back when she joined the operetta, well now she died, apparently… That's the story, my dear Pankrat… They sent me a letter…"

The toads bellowed mournfully, and the twilight was enrobing the professor. Here it was… the night. Moscow… white lamps turning on somewhere outside… Lost and miserable, Pankrat stood fearfully at attention, arms at his sides…

"Go on, Pankrat," the professor pronounced heavily and waved his hand. "Go to bed, my dearest friend Pankrat."

And the night fell. Pankrat ran out of the laboratory on tiptoes, ran to his tiny room, dug up an already opened bottle of bitter Russian vodka from a pile of rags in the corner, and gulped down an entire glass in one go. He followed it with some salted bread, and his eyes cheered up somewhat.

Late in the evening, close to midnight, Pankrat was sitting barefoot on a bench in the dimly lit vestibule and, scratching his chest beneath his calico shirt, he conversed with the sleepless bowler hat man on duty:

"I'd rather he killed me, by God…"

"Was he really crying?" the bowler asked curiously.

"By… Go…" Pankrat assured him.

"A great scientist," the bowler agreed. "Everyone knows a frog can't replace a wife."

"Never," Pankrat agreed.

Then he thought awhile and added:

"I'm thinking of bringing my old girl here… What good is it for her to sit around back in the village? Only she won't be able to stand all this vermin…"

"They are beyond disgusting, no doubt about it," the bowler agreed.

Not a single sound came from the scientist's laboratory. Nor was there any light inside. No strip under the door.

CHAPTER 8

★

THE INCIDENT AT THE STATE FARM

Truly, there is no time of the year more pleasant than late August in, say, the Smolensk Province. The summer of 1928 was an excellent one, as you know, with timely spring rains, with a full, hot sun, with an excellent harvest... Apples ripened in the former Sheremetev estate, the forests were full of green, the yellow squares of fields lay between them... A man looks better in the open country. And Alexander Semyonovich looked nowhere near as unpleasant as he did in the city. And he was not wearing the ugly jacket. A copper tan was on his face, his open calico shirt revealed a chest overgrown with very thick black hair, and he was wearing canvas pants. And his eyes took on a calmer, kinder look.

Alexander Semyonovich ran down spiritedly from the colonnaded porch with the sign: "RED RAY STATE FARM" beneath a red star, right towards the light truck that had delivered the three black chambers under guard.

He fussed around with his assistants the whole day, setting up the chambers in the former winter garden – the Sheremetevs' greenhouse... By evening, everything was ready. A frosted white sphere lit up beneath the glass ceiling, the chambers were set up on brick foundations, and the mechanic that had arrived with the chambers clicked and spun the shiny knobs and lit up the mysterious red ray on the asbestos floors of the black boxes.

Alexander Semyonovich fussed around, climbing up the ladder himself to check the wiring.

The next day, the very same light truck returned from the

station and spat out three crates made of excellent smooth
plywood, plastered over with tags and black labels with white
text:

VORSICHT: EIER!
CAUTION: EGGS!

"Why did they send so little?" wondered Alexander Semyonovich, but nevertheless he began to fuss right away, unpacking
the eggs. The unpacking was performed in the same greenhouse by Alexander Semyonovich himself, his incredibly fat
wife Manya, the Sheremetevs' one-eyed former gardener, now
working at the state farm in the universal position of groundskeeper, a guard who was forced to live at the farm, and the
maid Dunia. This was not Moscow, and everything here had
a simple, domestic, and friendly character. Alexander Semyonovich gave orders as he looked fondly at the crates, which
looked like valuable, compactly wrapped gift boxes beneath the
tender sunset light coming from the upper glass panes of the
greenhouse. The guard, whose rifle slumbered peacefully by
the doors, was removing staples and metal trim with a pair of
pliers. There was a cracking sound… dust came pouring. His
sandals flopping, Alexander Semyonovich fussed around the
crates.

"Take it easy, please," he said to the guard. "Careful. Can't
you see – it's eggs!"

"No worries," rasped the provincial warrior, drilling away,
"just a second…"

Tr-r-r… and the dust continued to pour.

The eggs had been packaged very well: beneath the wooden
lid was a layer of wax paper, then blotting paper, then a firmly
packed layer of wood shavings, then sawdust, and then the
white tips of the eggs began to appear.

"Foreign packed," Alexander Semyonovich said lovingly,
digging around in the sawdust, "not like ours. Careful, Manya,
you'll break them."

"You're nuts, Alexander Semyonovich," his wife replied. "What is this, gold? As if I haven't seen eggs before! Oh! Look how big they are!"

"Foreign," Alexander Semyonovich said, placing the eggs on a wooden table. "These aren't our meager peasant eggs... All from Brahmaputras, no doubt, may the devil take 'em! German..."

"You know it," the guard confirmed, admiring the eggs.

"I just don't understand why they are so dirty," Alexander Semyonovich said pensively. "Manya, look after this. Keep unpacking them, and I'm going to make a phone call."

And Alexander Semyonovich went to use the phone in the main office of the state farm, across the yard.

In the evening, the phone began to rattle in the laboratory of the zoological institute. Professor Persikov ruffled his hair and went to pick it up.

"Yes?" he asked.

"You have a call from the provinces," the receiver replied quietly in a hissing female voice.

"Very well. I'm listening," Persikov said distastefully into the black mouth of the telephone. Something clicked inside it, and then a concerned, distant male voice said into his ear:

"Should we wash the eggs, professor?"

"What's this? What? What did you ask me?" Persikov became irritated. "Where are you calling from?"

"From Nikolskoye, Smolensk Province," the receiver replied.

"I don't understand a thing. I have never heard of Nikolskoye. Who is this?"

"Phate," the receiver said sternly.

"What Phate? Oh, yes... it's you... so what were you asking?"

"Should we wash them? We received a shipment of chicken eggs from abroad..."

"And?"

"They are all filthy-like..."

"You are mixed up… How can they be 'filthy-like,' as you call it? Sure, there could be some… droppings stuck to them… or something else…"

"So we shouldn't wash them?"

"Of course not… Are you already loading the eggs into the chambers?"

"I'm loading them, yes," the receiver replied.

"Hmm," Persikov grumbled.

"So long," the receiver clicked and fell silent.

"'So long,'" Persikov repeated hatefully to private docent Ivanov. "How do you like this character, Pyotr Stepanovich?"

Ivanov laughed.

"That was him? I can imagine what he'll cook up with those eggs."

"F… f… f…" Persikov began angrily. "Imagine, Pyotr Stepanovich… Very well… it's quite possible that the ray will have the same effect on the deuteroplasm of the chicken egg as it did on the amphibian plasm. It's quite possible that he'll be able to hatch chickens… But neither you nor I can say what kind of chickens they'll be… maybe they'll be unfit for anything. Maybe they'll die off in two days. Maybe it won't be safe to eat them! Can I even vouch that they'll stand up straight? Maybe they'll have brittle bones." Persikov became excited, waving the palm of his hand and counting on his fingers.

"Exactly right," Ivanov agreed.

"Can you vouch that they will produce offspring, Pyotr Stepanovich? Perhaps this character is about to breed sterile chickens. He'll grow them the size of dogs, and then you can wait for a new generation until the second coming."

"It's impossible to vouch for it," Ivanov agreed.

"And what arrogance!" Persikov continued to work himself up. "What cheek! Note, moreover, that they charged me with providing that scoundrel with instructions," – Persikov gestured at the paper brought by Phate (it lay on the laboratory table) – "and how am I supposed to teach that ignoramus when I can't even say anything on this matter myself?"

"You could not refuse?" Ivanov asked.

Persikov grew purple, picked up the paper, and showed it to Ivanov. The latter read it and smirked sarcastically.

"Right," he said pointedly.

"And note, also… I have been waiting for my order for two months now, and there is no sign of it. He, meanwhile, received his eggs instantaneously, not to mention all kinds of support…"

"He won't get anywhere, Vladimir Ipatievich. And the chambers will simply end up back here."

"If only it were sooner rather than later, my experiments are being held up."

"Yes, it is most unfortunate. All of my preparations are complete."

"Did you receive the pressure suits?"

"Yes, this morning."

Persikov grew less agitated and began to brighten up.

"Uh-huh… I believe we should do as follows. We'll seal the doors of the operating room shut and open the window…"

"Of course," Ivanov agreed.

"Three helmets?"

"Three. Yes."

"Well, then… It'll be you, me, and we'll get one of the students. Give him the third helmet."

"Grinmuth, perhaps."

"That's the one you have working on the salamanders? Hmm… he is all right. Although, hold on, this spring he could not describe the structure of the swim bladder of *Gymnodontes*," Persikov recalled spitefully.

"No, he is all right… He is a good student," Ivanov came to the defense of his charge.

"We'll have to forgo sleep for a night," Persikov continued. "Only, Pyotr Stepanovich, please check the gas, because hell only knows with that Volunteer-Chem outfit. They could have sent us useless junk."

"No, no," Ivanov waved his arms, "I already tried it

yesterday. We have to give them credit, Vladimir Ipatievich, the gas is excellent."

"What did you try it on?"

"Ordinary toads. They die instantly as soon as you turn on the gas. Oh, and we should do one other thing, Vladimir Ipatievich. You should write a request to the GPU to send you an electric revolver."

"But I don't know how to use it…"

"I'll take care of it," Ivanov replied. "We tried one out on the Kliazma, just for fun… there was a GPU man living next to me there… An excellent gadget. And extremely simple to use… Fires silently, range is about a hundred paces, and kills on the spot. We shot at some crows… We wouldn't even need the gas, if you ask me."

"Hmm… that's a clever idea. Very clever." Persikov walked to the corner of the room, picked up the receiver, and croaked:

"Get me, what's her face… Lubyanka…"

* * *

The days were extremely hot. The thick, transparent heat was clearly visible as it shimmered over the fields. And the nights were magical, green, deceiving. The moon shone over the former Sheremetev estate, making it look inexpressibly beautiful. The state farm palace glowed as if made of sugar, the shadows trembled in the garden, and the ponds took on a two-tone hue – half lit by slanted pillars of moonlight, half plunged in bottomless dark. The spots of moonlight were so bright that one could easily read *Izvestiya* in them, except for the chess section, set in small nonpareil type. But, of course, no one read *Izvestiya* on nights like these… The maid Dunia somehow ended up in the grove located behind the farm, and, by way of coincidence, the red-mustached driver of the battered farm truck appeared there as well. It is unclear what they were doing there. They huddled in the faint shadow of an elm, right on the driver's coat draped on the ground. A lamp burned in the kitchen, where two gardeners were having dinner, while Madam Phate was sitting on the colonnaded veranda in a white housecoat and fantasizing as she gazed at the beautiful moon.

At ten o'clock, when the village of Kontsovka, located behind the state farm, fell silent, the charming sounds of a flute began to drift over the idyllic setting. It defied description how natural these sounds felt over the groves and the columns of the Sheremetevs' former palace. The voice of the fragile Lisa from "The Queen of Spades" blended into a duet with the voice of the passionate Polina[1] and soared into the moonlit sky, like a vision of an old and yet infinitely dear regime, charming to the point of tears.

"Fading… Fading…" the flute whistled, trilling and sighing.

The groves stood still, and Dunia listened, fatal like a forest nymph, placing her cheek against the coarse, red-haired, manly cheek of the driver.

"Son of a bitch ain't too bad at pipin'," said the driver, hugging Dunia's waist with his manly hand.

The flute player was none other than the manager of the state farm, Alexander Semyonovich Phate, and, to give him credit, he played it magnificently. In fact, the flute has once been Alexander Semyonovich's profession. Up until 1917, he played in the famous concert ensemble of maestro Petukhov, which gathered every evening in the cozy "Magic Dreams" movie theater in the city of Yekaterinoslavl, gracing the foyer with harmonious sounds. But the great year of 1917, which radically altered the careers of many people, led Alexander Semyonovich down a new path as well. He left behind "Magic Dreams" and the dusty, star-spangled satin of its foyer, and dashed headlong into the open sea of war and revolution, trading in his flute for a lethal Mauser. The waves tossed him around for a long time,

1 The duet of Lisa and Polina is in the 2nd act of Tchaikovsky's opera "The Queen of Spades."

washing him ashore in the Crimea, in Moscow, in Turkestan, and even in Vladivostok. It took a revolution to fully realize Alexander Semyonovich's potential. It turned out that he was really a great man, and that his place was, of course, not in the foyer of "Magic Dreams." Without getting bogged down in details, let us just say that 1927 and the beginning of 1928 found Alexander Semyonovich in Turkestan, where he was the editor of a very large paper and also, as a member of the local Supreme Agricultural Commission, gained fame for his incredible work in the irrigation of the Turkestan region. In 1928, Phate arrived in Moscow and was granted some well-deserved rest. The Supreme Commission of a certain party, whose membership card the old-fashioned, provincial man carried proudly in his pocket, had relieved him and appointed him to a quiet, honorary post. But alas! Alas! To the great misfortune of the republic, Alexander Semyonovich's vigorous mind did not settle down, and in Moscow Phate came across Persikov's invention. In his room at the "Red Paris" hotel on Tverskaya, Alexander Semyonovich came up with the idea to revive the fowl industry in the republic within a month. The Agricultural Commission listened to Phate, agreed with him, and then Phate came to the eccentric zoologist with the thick paper in hand.

The musical performance over the glassy ponds, the groves, and the garden was already nearing its end, but then something happened that interrupted it even sooner. Namely, the dogs in Kontsovka, which should have been sleeping already, erupted suddenly in unbearable barking that transitioned gradually into a torturous communal howl. Growing stronger, the howling raced over the fields, and suddenly a crackling, million-strong chorus of frogs in the ponds began to croak in response. It was all so eerie that it even seemed for a moment that the mysterious, magical night had begun to fade away.

Alexander Semyonovich put down his flute and walked out on the veranda.

"Did you hear that, Manya? Those damn dogs... What do you think got into them?"

"How should I know?" asked Manya, gazing at the moon.

"Manya, what do you say we go take a look at the eggs?" Alexander Semyonovich offered.

"Good lord, Alexander Semyonovich, you've gone completely nuts with your eggs and your chickens. Take a break for a little bit!"

"No, Manechka, let's go."

The bright electrical sphere burned in the greenhouse. Dunia appeared as well, her face glowing and her eyes sparkling. Alexander Semyonovich gently opened the observation windows, and they glanced inside the chambers. Spotted eggs tinted with bright red light lay in neat rows on the white asbestos floors, and the chambers were silent. The 15,000 candlepower light hissed quietly overhead.

"Oh, I'll hatch those chicks!" Alexander Semyonovich spoke with enthusiasm, gazing into the observation slots on the sides and the broad ventilation ports on the tops of the chambers. "You'll see... What? You think I won't?"

"You know, Alexander Semyonovich," Dunia said, smiling, "the peasants in Kontsovka say you are the antichrist. They say your eggs are the devil's. That it's a sin to hatch them in a machine. Wanted to kill you, even."

Alexander Semyonovich shuddered and looked at his wife. His face turned yellow.

"Would you listen to that? Those people! What are you going to do with those people? Huh? Manechka, we'll have to call a meeting... I'll invite officials from the district office tomorrow. I'll give a speech. We'll have to do a bit of work around here... It's a real backwater place..."

"Ignorance," said the guard, sitting on his overcoat near the door of the greenhouse.

The following day was marked with very strange and inexplicable events. In the morning, at the first ray of sunlight, the groves that usually greeted the luminary with a powerful and incessant twittering of birds met it with complete silence. Absolutely everyone noticed this. It was just like before a thunderstorm, only there was no sign of an impending thunderstorm. The conversations in the farm took on a strange and – to Alexander Semyonovich – equivocal tone, especially since a known rabble-rouser and local sage from Kontsovka, nicknamed Goat Wen, had claimed that apparently all the birds had gathered into flocks and flown somewhere north, the hell out of the Sheremetev estate. This was just plain silly. Alexander Semyonovich grew very upset and spent the whole day trying to get in touch with the town of Grachevka. They promised him to send two speakers in a couple of days – one to discuss international affairs and one to speak about Volunteer-Fowl.

The evening was also not without its surprises. The groves had fallen silent in the morning, showing quite clearly how suspicious and unpleasant silent trees can be; at midday, the sparrows had disappeared somewhere from the state farm yard; but in the evening, the pond at the Sheremetev estate had fallen silent. This was truly astounding, for everyone in a twenty-five mile radius knew about the famous chattering of the Sheremetev frogs. And now, it was as though they had died out. Not a single sound came from the pond, and the sedge stood silent. One must admit that this made Alexander Semyonovich utterly upset. People had begun to talk about the strange events in a most unpleasant fashion – that is, behind Alexander Semyonovich's back.

"It really is strange," Alexander Semyonovich said to his wife at dinner. "I don't understand what possessed those birds to fly away."

"How should I know?" Manya replied. "Maybe they flew away from your ray."

"You're a regular fool, Manya," Alexander Semyonovich said, dropping his spoon, "just like those peasants. What's the ray got to do with it?"

"I don't know. Leave me alone."

Late in the evening came a third surprise – the dogs began howling again in Kontsovka, and how! Their incessant moaning and their angry, mournful whines spread through the moonlit fields.

Alexander Semyonovich's reward was yet another surprise, this time a pleasant one, in the greenhouse. The chambers were filled with a continuous tapping coming from inside the red eggs. "Tocky... tocky... tocky... tocky..." came from one egg after another.

The tapping inside the eggs was a triumph for Alexander Semyonovich. All the strange occurrences in the groves and in the pond were forgotten at once. Everyone converged on the greenhouse: Manya, Dunia, the groundskeeper, and the guard, who had left his rifle by the door.

"Well? What have you got to say?" Alexander Semyonovich asked victoriously. Everyone leaned curiously towards the doors of the first chamber.

"That's the beaks of them chicks tapping," Alexander Semyonovich continued, beaming. "You say I won't hatch them chicks? No, my darlings," he said, slapping the guard on the shoulder from an excess of emotion, "I'll hatch chicks that'll make you gasp. Now we'll have to keep our eyes peeled," he added strictly. "As soon as they begin to hatch, you let me know at once."

"All right," the groundskeeper, Dunia, and the guard replied in unison.

"Tacky... tacky... tacky..." erupted from one egg after another in the first chamber. Indeed, the sight of newborn life inside the thin, shimmering shells was so interesting that the entire company sat on overturned empty boxes for a long time, gazing at the crimson eggs ripening in the mysterious, glimmering light. They went to bed rather late, when the greenish night had already poured over the state farm and its surroundings. The night was mysterious and perhaps even frightening, probably because its complete silence was repeatedly broken by the unreasonable, utterly miserable whining and howling of the dogs in Kontsovka. No one knew what had got into the damn dogs.

In the morning, trouble was waiting for Alexander Semyonovich. The guard was extremely embarrassed, placing his hands
on his heart and swearing to God that he did not fall asleep, but
nevertheless saw nothing.

"It's a mystery," the guard insisted, "I am not to blame here,
comrade Phate."

"Thank you from the bottom of my heart, much obliged,"
Alexander Semyonovich scolded him. "What were you thinking, comrade? Why do you think we put you here? To guard.
So tell me, where did they go? They hatched, no? Which means
they escaped. Which means you left the door open and left
your post. I want my chicks!"

"I have nowhere to leave. What, you think I don't know my
job?" the warrior took offense at last. "Why do you accuse me
for nothing, comrade Phate?"

"So where'd they go?"

"How should I know?" the warrior grew exasperated.
"How am I supposed to keep track of them? Why am I here?
To watch so no one makes off with your chambers, and I am
doing my job. The chambers are here. Ain't no law that says
I have to catch your chicks for you. Who knows what chicks
you're going to hatch in there, maybe you won't even be able to
catch them on a bicycle!"

Alexander Semyonovich was somewhat taken aback; he
grumbled something else and fell into a state of bewilderment.
The situation was indeed strange. In chamber number one, which
was the first to be loaded, two eggs at the very source of the ray
had been broken. And one of them had even rolled aside. The
broken eggshells lay on the asbestos floor, illuminated by the ray.

"Hell knows," Alexander Semyonovich muttered. "The windows are locked, and they couldn't have flown away through
the roof, after all!"

He flung back his head and looked at the several large openings in the glass framework of the roof.

"What are you talking about, Alexander Semyonovich?"
Dunia said with great astonishment. "As if chicks are going to

fly. They are here somewhere… Chuck… chuck… chuck…"
she began to call, peeking into the corners of the greenhouse,
which were piled full of dusty flower planters, boards, and various
ous rubbish. But no chicks responded.

The entire staff ran around the yard for a good two hours
trying to find the lively chicks, but no one saw anything. The
day passed in great excitement. The guard was bolstered by
the groundskeeper, who was also ordered to look into the
viewports of the chambers every fifteen minutes and report
to Alexander Semyonovich if anything happened. The guard
sat by the doors and scowled, holding his rifle between his
knees. Alexander Semyonovich lost himself completely in the
commotion and only had lunch at two o'clock. After lunch, he
napped for an hour in the cool shade on Sheremetev's former
ottoman, had a drink of farm-brewed kvass[2], stopped by the
greenhouse, and made sure that everything was in order. The
elderly groundskeeper lay on his stomach atop some matting
and stared, blinking, into the viewport of the first chamber.
The guard was alert, never leaving the doors.

But there were also new developments: the eggs in the
third chamber, which was the last to be loaded, began to make
smacking, clicking noises, as if something was sobbing inside.

"Oh, they're brewing," Alexander Semyonovich said.
"They're a-brewing, I can see now. Hear that?" he said to the
guard.

"Yes, fascinating," the latter replied in a very equivocal tone,
shaking his head.

Alexander Semyonovich squatted by the chambers for a
little bit, but nothing hatched in his presence, so he got up,
stretched, and announced that he was not leaving the estate
but merely going for a swim in the pond, and that he was to
be summoned immediately if something happened. He ran to
the bedroom in the palace, where two narrow spring beds with
crumpled linen were standing next to a pile of green apples

---

2 *Kvass* – A fermented beverage made with rye bread.

and mounds of millet intended for future hatchlings, and equipped himself with a shaggy towel. After a brief thought, he also took his flute in order to spend some of his free time playing by the smooth water. He ran out of the palace briskly, crossed the yard of the state farm, and headed down the willow alley towards the pond. Phate was walking at a brisk pace, waving his towel, his flute tucked under his arm. The heat poured from the sky through the willow branches, and his body ached and begged to be immersed in water. A thicket of burdocks appeared on his right, and he spat into it as he passed. And immediately, a rustling came from the depths of the sprawled, tangled greenery, as if someone was dragging a log. Feeling a brief, unpleasant prickle in his heart, Alexander Semyonovich turned towards the thicket and looked at it in surprise. The pond had not produced any sounds for two days now. The rustling stopped, and the smooth surface of the pond appeared invitingly over the burdocks, along with the gray roof of the bathing house. Several dragonflies dashed in front of Alexander Semyonovich. He was about to head towards the planked walkway leading to the water when the rustling from the greenery came again, this time joined by a quick hissing, as if steam and oil were escaping from an engine. Alexander Semyonovich pricked up his ears and looked deeper into the thick wall of weeds.

"Alexander Semyonovich," the voice of Phate's wife called out just then, and her white blouse flashed, disappeared, and then flashed again in the raspberry bushes. "Wait for me, I'll go for a swim too."

His wife was hurrying to the pond, but Alexander Semyonovich did not respond, his attention locked on the burdocks. A grayish-olive log began to rise from the depths, growing before his eyes. The log was covered by what looked to Alexander Semyonovich like wet, yellowish spots. It began to stretch, bending and shifting, and it grew taller than a short, crooked willow... Then the top part of the log developed a kink, leaned down slightly, and something roughly the height of a Moscow lamppost began to loom over Alexander Semyonovich. Only this something was about three times wider than a lamppost and much prettier due to its scaly pattern. Not understanding a thing but feeling a chill, Alexander Semyonovich looked at the top of the hideous post, and his heart stopped beating for several seconds. It seemed to him that the August day has suddenly turned very frosty, and his eyes darkened, as if he were staring at the sun through a pair of his summer pants.

There was a head on the top end of the log. It was a sharp, flat head, decorated with a round yellow spot on an olive background. Icy narrow eyes sat in the roof of the head, open and lacking eyelids, and these eyes glimmered with absolutely incredible hatred. The head made a rapid movement, as if pecking at the air, and the log crawled back into the burdocks, leaving only the eyes to stare at Alexander Semyonovich. Covered in sticky sweat, the latter could only manage four incomprehensible words, brought on by mind-numbing fear – so peachy were these eyes in the leaves:

"Is this a joke…"

Then he recalled that fakirs… yes… yes… in India… a woven basket and a picture… snake-charmers.

The head soared up once more, and the body began to emerge. Alexander Semyonovich raised the flute to his lips, squeaked hoarsely, and began to play the waltz from "Eugene Onegin," running out of breath every other second. The eyes in the greenery immediately lit up with insatiable hatred towards that opera.

"Have you gone nuts, playing in this heat?" came Manya's cheerful voice, and Alexander Semyonovich perceived a white spot somewhere on the right out of the corner of his eye.

Then a blood-curdling scream pierced the entire farm, growing and rising, and the waltz began to limp as if on broken legs. The head in the greenery lunged forward, its eyes abandoning Alexander Semyonovich and leaving his soul to repentance. The snake, about twelve yards long and as thick as a man, leaped from the burdock like a spring. A cloud of dust splashed onto the path, and the waltz halted. The snake flew right past the manager of the farm to where the white blouse had appeared on the path. Phate could see it with perfect clarity: Manya turned a pale yellow color, and her long hair rose a foot above her head, as if made of wire. Right before Phate's eyes, the snake opened its maw for an instant, revealing something resembling a fork, grasped Manya's shoulder with its teeth as she sank down into the dust, and jerked her a yard above the ground. Then Manya repeated her piercing deathly scream. The snake twisted into a twelve-yard corkscrew, kicking up a whirl-wind with its tail, and began to crush Manya. She did not make another sound, and Phate could only hear her bones snap-ping. Her head soared high above the ground, pressed tenderly against the cheek of the snake. Blood splashed from Manya's mouth, her broken arm popped out from the coils, and little fountains of blood sprayed from under her fingernails. Then the snake unhinged its jaw, flung its maw wide open, and cov-ered Manya's head all at once, and began to slide over her body like a glove sliding onto a finger. The breath emanating from the snake in all directions was so hot that Phate felt it on his face, while the tail nearly swept him off the path into the acrid dust. It was then that Phate's hair turned gray. First the left, and then the right side of his black head broke out in silver. Nause-ated to death, he managed to tear himself away from the path and, seeing nothing and no one else, began to run, his savage screams echoing through the surroundings…

CHAPTER 9

★

THE LIVING MASS

The agent of the State Political Administration at Dugino Station, Schukin, was a very brave man. He said pensively to his colleague, the red-haired Polaitis:

"Well, let's go, then. Eh? Get the motorcycle." He was silent for a moment and then addressed the man sitting on the bench: "You ought to put down that flute."

But the shaking, gray-haired man sitting on the bench in the Dugino GPU did not put down his flute, and instead began weeping and moaning. Then Schukin and Polaitis realized they would have to extract the flute. The man's fingers appeared glued to it. Schukin, who possessed enormous, almost circus-like strength, began to peel away finger after finger until he got them all. The flute was then placed on the table.

It was the early, sunny morning of the day after Manya's death.

"You'll come with us," Schukin said, turning to Alexander Semyonovich, "show us what happened and where." But Phate shrank away from him in terror and covered his face with his hands, as if shielding himself from a horrible vision.

"You have to show us," Polaitis added sternly.

"No, leave him alone. The man is not himself right now."

"Send me to Moscow," Alexander Semyonovich asked, weeping.

"You aren't going back to the state farm at all?"

But Phate shielded himself with his hands again instead of replying, and horror began to pour from his eyes.

"All right," Schukin decided. "You really are out of sorts… I see that. The express train is leaving shortly, you can take it."

Then, while the station keeper was giving water to Alexander Semyonovich and the teeth of the latter were clattering on the chipped blue mug, Schukin and Polaitis had a conference… Polaitis believed that nothing had happened, and that Phate was merely insane and had experienced a horrible hallucination. Schukin, meanwhile, leaned towards the idea that a boa constrictor may have escaped from the town of Grachevka, where a circus was presently on tour. Hearing their doubting whispers, Phate got up. He had come to his senses somewhat, and, spreading his arms like a Biblical prophet, he said:

"Listen to me. Listen. How can you not believe me? It was there. Where is my wife?"

Schukin became silent and serious and immediately sent some sort of telegram to Grachevka. He ordered a third agent to stay at Alexander Semyonovich's side at all times and to accompany him to Moscow. Meanwhile, Schukin and Polaitis began to prepare for a mission. They had only one electric revolver, but this alone was good protection. The fifty-round 1927 model, pride of French close combat technology, had a range of only a hundred paces but produced a field two meters in diameter and killed every living thing within that field on the spot. It was very difficult to miss. Schukin strapped on the shiny electric toy, while Polaitis took a regular 25-round submachine gun and a few clips, and together they got on a single motorcycle and rode off through the chilly, dewy morning down the road leading to the state farm. The motorcycle rattled off the thirteen miles separating the station from the farm in a quarter of an hour (Phate had walked the entire night, hiding every few moments in the roadside grass in deathly fear), and when the sun had already begun to heat up considerably, the colonnaded sugar palace appeared in the greenery on the hill overlooking the winding Bog River. A deathly silence reigned here. Right by the entrance to the farm, the agents passed by a peasant on a cart. He was drifting along leisurely, loaded with sacks, and they soon left him behind. The motorcycle flew over the bridge, and Polaitis sounded the horn to call somebody. But no one replied, except for frenzied, distant dogs over in Kontsovka. Slowing down, the motorcycle drove up to the gates with the verdigris lions. The dusty agents in yellow gaiters dismounted, secured the bike to the grated fence using a lock and chain, and entered the courtyard. The silence stunned them.

"Hey, anyone there?" Schukin yelled loudly.

But no one responded to his deep voice. The agents circled the courtyard, growing more and more surprised. Polaitis frowned. Schukin began to look around more seriously, knitting his fair eyebrows. They glanced into the kitchen through the open window and saw no one there, but the entire floor was littered with the white pieces of broken dishes.

"You know, something did happen here. I can see it now. Some kind of catastrophe," Polaitis spoke.

"Hey, anyone here? Hey!" Schukin shouted, but the echo from the vaults of the kitchen was his only response.

"Who the hell knows what happened here!" Schukin grumbled. "It couldn't have eaten them all at once, after all. Or maybe they just ran away. Let's go into the house."

The door of the palace with the colonnaded veranda was wide open, and the building itself was completely empty. The agents even went as far as the attic, knocking on all the doors and opening each one, but it was all in vain. They walked outside once more through the deserted porch.

"We'll go around, to the greenhouse," Schukin ordered. "We'll search everything, and then we can make a phone call."

The agents walked down the brick path, past the flowerbeds, towards the back yard. They crossed it and saw the shiny windows of the greenhouse.

"Wait a second," Schukin said in a whisper and unholstered his revolver. Polaitis pricked up his ears and removed the submachine gun from his back. A strange and very loud noise came from the greenhouse and somewhere beyond it. It sounded like the hissing of a steam engine. "Zau-zau… zau-zau… s-s-s-s-s…" hissed the greenhouse.

"Careful, now," Schukin whispered, and, trying not to make loud footsteps, the agents walked right up to the glass and peeked inside the greenhouse.

Polaitis shrank back right away, and his face turned pale. Schukin's mouth fell open, and he froze with the revolver in his hand.

The entire greenhouse was alive: a writhing, wormlike mass. Weaving together into giant clumps and disentangling, hissing and uncurling, slithering and swaying their heads, enormous snakes were crawling on the floor. Broken eggshells lay everywhere, crackling under their bodies. A pale, extremely powerful electric lamp shone on the ceiling, casting the entire inside of the greenhouse in a strange cinematic light. Three enormous dark boxes that looked like cameras lay on the floor; two of them had been pushed aside and tilted, and were dark, but a small, deep-crimson spot of light glimmered in the third. Snakes of all sizes crawled on the wires, climbed up the frame of the greenhouse, and slithered through the openings in the roof. A very dark spotted snake several yards long was hanging on the electric lamp itself, its head swaying beneath the lamp like a pendulum. Various rattling noises could be heard through the hissing, and a strange, putrid smell drifted from the greenhouse, resembling a stagnant pond. And finally the agents hazily saw numerous white eggs piled in the dusty corners, as well as a strange, gigantic, long-legged bird lying motionlessly near the chambers and the body of a man in gray by the door, next to a rifle.

"Get back," Schukin shouted and began to retreat, pushing Polaitis away with his left hand and raising the revolver with his right. He managed to squeeze off around nine shots, each expelling a hissing, greenish bolt of lightning into the greenhouse. The noise grew tremendously, and the entire greenhouse stirred into frenzied motion in response to Schukin's fire. Flat reptilian heads began to flicker in every opening. The rumbling immediately spread through the entire farm, reflecting from the walls. "Chuh-chuh-chuh-chuh," Polaitis fired his gun as he backed away. A strange, four-legged rustling came from behind him, and suddenly Polaitis let out a horrible cry and fell flat. A brownish-green creature on splayed legs, with an enormous pointed snout and a ridged tail, resembling an enormous lizard, had glided from around the corner of a shed; it bit fiercely through Polaitis's leg, throwing him to the ground.

"Help!" Polaitis shouted, and immediately his left hand slipped into the creature's maw and made a crunching sound; trying in vain to get up, he dragged the revolver in his right hand along the ground. Schukin turned around and panicked. He managed to squeeze off a shot, but it went wide because he was afraid to kill his colleague. His next shot was directed at the greenhouse, because an enormous olive snake head emerged suddenly between smaller heads and the body lunged straight for him. He managed to kill the gigantic snake with the shot and went back to jumping and spinning around Polaitis, who was already half-dead in the crocodile's maw, trying to find a way to shoot and kill the horrible monster without harming the agent. Finally, he managed to do it. The electric revolver clapped twice, illuminating everything around it with greenish light, and the crocodile twitched, stretched out, and stiffened, releasing Polaitis. Blood was pouring from the agent's sleeve and mouth, and he was pulling his broken left leg along, leaning on his intact right arm. His eyes were fading.

"Schukin... run," he groaned, sobbing.

Schukin fired several times in the direction of the greenhouse, knocking out several windows. But then an enormous, flexible, olive-colored spring uncoiled from a basement window behind him, slithered across the yard, its twelve-yard body stretching along its entire length, and wound around Schukin's legs in a split second. He was tossed on the ground, and the shiny revolver tumbled away. Schukin screamed loudly, then choked, and the coils enveloped him completely save for the head. A coil passed over his head, tearing off the scalp, and the head cracked. Not a single shot rang out after that on the farm. The hissing, omnipresent noise drowned everything else out. And the wind brought a very distant howl from Kontsovka in response, but now it was impossible to say whether it was canine or human.

CHAPTER 10

★

CATASTROPHE

Lights burned brightly in the night editorial office of the *Izvestiya* newspaper, and a portly issuing editor was proofing the second column of telegraphed news "Across the Union of Republics" on a lead table. A single galley caught his eye; he peered at it through his pince-nez and then burst out in laughter. He summoned the proofreaders from their office, as well as the maker-up, and showed the galley to everyone. The narrow strip of damp paper read:

> "Grachevka, Smolensk Province. A chicken with the size and kicking power of a horse has been spotted in the district. It has ladylike bourgeois feathers for a tail."

The typesetters laughed uproariously.

"In my time," said the issuing editor, giggling plentifully, "back when I was working for Vanya Sytin at *The Russian Word*, we'd drink until we saw elephants. That's the truth. And now, it seems, they make it till ostriches."

The typesetters laughed.

"An ostrich, of course," said the maker-up. "So shall we put it in, Ivan Bonifatievich?"

"Are you nuts?" replied the issuing editor. "I'm amazed the secretary let it through. It's just a drunken prank."

"Lads must have been celebrating something," the typesetters agreed, and the maker-up removed the notice about the ostrich from the table.

As a result, *Izvestiya* was released the next day with loads of interesting material, as usual, but without any mention of the Grachevka ostrich. Private docent Ivanov, who read *Izvestiya* studiously, folded up the newspaper in his office, yawned, declared: "Nothing interesting," and began to put on his white coat. A short while later, burners were lit in his laboratory, and frogs began to croak. As for Professor Persikov's laboratory, it was an utter mess. A frightened Pankrat was standing at attention, arms at his sides.

"Understood… yessir," he was saying.

Persikov handed him a wax-sealed envelope and said:

"Go right to the head of the livestock-rearing department, that Birdov, and tell him straight out that he is a swine. Tell him that Professor Persikov said so. And give him the envelope."

"Nice little errand…" thought the pale Pankrat and disappeared with the envelope.

Persikov fumed.

"Hell alone knows what this is," he whimpered, walking around the laboratory and rubbing his gloved hands together. "This is an unprecedented mockery of me and of zoology in general. These accursed chicken eggs are being delivered by the boxful, whereas I cannot get necessary supplies for two months now. As if America is that far away! Always disorder, always a mess." He began to count on his fingers: "The capture would take… at most ten days… okay, fifteen… all right, twenty, and two days by airplane, another day from London to Berlin. Berlin is six hours from here… this is an unspeakable outrage!"

He rushed fiercely at the telephone and began to call somewhere.

The laboratory had been fully prepared for mysterious and very dangerous experiments. There were strips of paper to seal the doors, diving helmets with circulation hoses, and several gas cylinders, shining like mercury, labeled: "Volunteer-Chem, do not touch," with images of skulls and crossbones.

It took at least three hours for the professor to calm down and busy himself with various small tasks. That was exactly what he did. He worked in the institute until eleven o'clock at night, and therefore learned nothing of what had transpired beyond the cream-colored walls. He did not hear about the odd rumor spreading through Moscow about some kind of snakes, or the shouts about a strange telegram in the evening paper, because the docent Ivanov was at the theater watching "Tsar Fyodor Ioannovich[1]," and as a result there was no one around to give the professor the news.

Persikov arrived on Prechistenka at around midnight and went to bed after reading some British article in the *Zoology Herald* journal that he had received from London. He slept, and so did the rest of the late-night city of Moscow, and only a giant gray building on Tverskaya St. was awake, shaking from the awful rumbling of the rotary presses belonging to *Izvestiya*. Incredible commotion and confusion reigned in the office of the issuing editor. He was dashing back and forth, utterly crazed, his eyes red, not knowing what to do, and kept telling everyone to go to hell. The maker-up followed him around with wine on his breath, saying:

"So what, Ivan Bonifatievich? It's no big deal. They can print an extra supplement tomorrow morning. We can't rip the paper out of the machines, can we now?"

Instead of going home, the typesetters walked around in droves, gathering in small groups and reading the telegrams which kept arriving throughout the whole night, every quarter hour, each one stranger and more monstrous than the last. The pointed hat of Alfred Bronsky flickered in the blinding pink light flooding the printing office. And the fat mechanical man creaked and hobbled around, appearing here and there. The front doors kept slamming, and reporters came and went all through the night. All the twelve telephones in the printing office rang without pause, and the switchboard automatically sent busy signals in response to the mysterious new calls, and the signal horns kept singing and singing in front of the sleepless ladies at the switchboard...

---

1 A historical drama by Aleksey Tolstoy.

The typesetters plastered around the fat mechanical man, and the seafaring captain said:

"They'll have to send airplanes with gas."

"No doubt," the typesetters replied. "Look at what's happening." Then horrendous cursing rolled through the air, and someone's squealing voice shouted:

"That Persikov ought to be shot."

"What does Persikov have to do with it?" someone replied from the crowd. "That son of a bitch at the state farm – that's who ought to be shot."

"They should have put a guard on it," someone else shouted.

"Maybe it's not the eggs at all."

The rotary machines made the entire building shake and hum, and it seemed like the unattractive gray building was ablaze with electrical fire.

The new day did not put an end to its activity. On the contrary, the activity only increased, even though the electrical lights were turned off. Motorcycles rolled into the asphalted courtyard one by one, interspersed with cars. All of Moscow got up and dressed itself in the white sheets of newspaper, resembling birds. The sheets spilled and rustled in everyone's hands, and by eleven o'clock the news vendors were running out of issues, even though *Izvestiya* had a print run of a million and a half copies every day that month. Professor Persikov left Prechistenka on a bus and arrived at the institute. A new development awaited him there. Wooden crates reinforced with metal strips had been lined up carefully in the vestibule, numbering three in total and plastered in foreign labels in German, with a single Russian inscription in chalk on the top: "Caution: eggs."

The professor was overjoyed.

"Finally!" he exclaimed. "Pankrat, open the crates right away, and be careful not to break anything. Bring everything to my laboratory."

Pankrat carried out the order immediately, and in a quarter hour the laboratory, littered with wood shavings and pieces of paper, was filled with the professor's raging voice:

"Are they taunting me?" the professor howled, shaking his fists and turning the eggs in his hands. "That Birdov is a filthy animal. I won't be mocked. What is this, Pankrat?"

"Eggs, sir," Pankrat replied miserably.

"Chicken eggs, understand? Chicken eggs, may they rot in hell! What the hell am I going to do with them? Let that scoundrel from the state farm have them!"

Persikov dashed to the corner towards the telephone, but he did not have time to make a call.

"Vladimir Ipatievich! Vladimir Ipatievich!" Ivanov's voice thundered in the hallway of the institute.

Persikov turned away from the phone, while Pankrat shot off to the side, making way for the private docent. Contrary to his gentlemanly custom, the latter ran into the study without removing his gray hat, which remained planted on the back of his head. He was holding a newspaper sheet.

"Do you know what happened, Vladimir Ipatievich?" he shouted, waving the sheet in front of Persikov's face. The sheet was labeled: "Extra Supplement," and right in the center was a bright color photograph.

"No, just listen to what they've done," Persikov shouted in response without listening. "They think they can surprise me with chicken eggs. This Birdov is a real idiot, just look!"

Ivanov was absolutely stunned. He stared at the open boxes in horror, then at the sheet, and then his eyes nearly jumped out of their sockets.

"So that's what happened," he muttered, out of breath. "Now I understand... No, Vladimir Ipatievich, just look at this." He unfolded the sheet in an instant and pointed out the color photo to Persikov with trembling fingers. In the photo, an olive-colored snake with yellow spots was slithering through blurry greenery, resembling a hideous fire hose. The photo was taken from above, from a light airplane gliding precariously over the snake. "What do you think this is, Vladimir Ipatievich?"

Persikov moved his glasses to his forehead, then back to his eyes. He peered at the photo and said with great surprise:

"What the hell? That's… yes, that's an anaconda… a water boa constrictor…"

Ivanov threw off his hat, sank down on a chair, and said, banging out every word on the table with his fist:

"Vladimir Ipatievich, this anaconda is from the Smolensk Province. It's something monstrous. Do you understand? That scoundrel bred snakes instead of chickens and, as you can see, they produced the same phenomenal results as the frogs!"

"What's that?" Persikov replied, and his face turned gray. "You are joking, Pyotr Stepanovich… How?"

Ivanov was dumbstruck for a second, then regained the gift of speech and, thrusting his finger at the open box, where the white heads of the eggs peeked through yellow sawdust, said:

"That's how."

"Wha-a-at??" Persikov howled, beginning to comprehend. Ivanov waved his two clenched fists very confidently and shouted:

"As we are standing here. They sent your order for snake and ostrich eggs to the state farm, and you got the chicken eggs by mistake."

"Good god… good god…" Persikov replied, turning green, and began to sink onto the revolving stool.

Pankrat stood by the door in a stupor, pale and dumbfounded. Ivanov jumped up, grabbed the sheet, and, underscoring a line with his sharp fingernail, shouted into the professor's ears:

"Oh, they'll have a fun time now! I cannot even imagine what's going to happen. Just look, Vladimir Ipatievich," he screamed, reading the first words his eyes had landed on: "The snakes are advancing on Mozhaisk in droves… laying inordinate amounts of eggs. Eggs have been seen in the Dukhovsky district… Crocodiles and ostriches have appeared. Special purpose units… and state police detachments managed to stop the panic in Viazma after they set the local forest on fire, halting the advance of the reptiles…"

Colors changing every second on his face, a pale blue Persikov got up from the stool with frenzied eyes and, gasping for air, began to scream:

"Anaconda... anaconda... a water boa! Good god!" Neither Ivanov nor Pankrat had ever seen him in such a state.

The professor ripped of his necktie in one motion, tearing off the buttons on his shirt. He turned a horrible, paralytic purple color, and, swaying, with utterly vacant, glassy eyes, dashed out of the room. His screams echoed beneath the stone vaults of the institute.

"Anaconda... anaconda..." thundered the echo.

"Go after the professor!" Ivanov squealed at Pankrat, who was dancing on the spot in horror. "Get him water... he's having a stroke."

Chapter 11

★

Battle and Death

A feverish electric night blazed throughout Moscow. All the lights were on, and the apartments were full of shining lamps with their shades removed. Not a single man, excepting the youngest children, was asleep in Moscow, which had a population of four million. The people in the apartments ate and drank whatever came to hand. The people in the apartments kept shouting something, and contorted faces looked out of the windows on all the floors every other minute, gazing at the sky, which was sliced in every direction by projector beams. White lights kept flashing in the sky, lighting up Moscow with flying white cones and fading and disappearing. The sky hummed incessantly with the very low rumbling of airplanes. It was especially frightening around Tverskaya-Yamskaya. Trains arrived every ten minutes at Alexandrovsky Station, constructed haphazardly from freight cars, passenger cars of every class, and even cistern cars, completely plastered over with crazed people. People ran down Tverskaya-Yamskaya in thick masses, rode the buses, and traveled on the roofs of streetcars, crushing each other and falling under the wheels. The alarming, crackling sound of gunshots kept flaring up above the crowd at the train station – military units were trying to put an end to the panic of madmen running along the railway tracks from the Smolensk Province towards Moscow. Panes of glass kept bursting with frenzied, flimsy, sniveling sounds at the train station, and all the steam engines were howling. All the streets were littered with posters that had been tossed and trampled underfoot, and the same posters stared from all the walls, lit up by hot crimson reflectors. Everyone already knew what they said, and no one read them. They announced that martial law had been declared in Moscow. They threatened consequences for spreading panic and informed that detachments of the Red Army were already on their way to the Smolensk Province, unit after unit, equipped with gas. But the posters could not halt the howling night. The people in the apartments kept dropping and smashing dishes and flowerpots, they ran around, bumping into things, they packed and unpacked various bundles and suitcases in the vain hope of making it to Kalanchevskaya Square, or to the Yaroslavsky or Nikolayevsky train stations. Alas, all the train stations leading north and east had been surrounded by very dense cordons of infantry. Enormous trucks, their chains swaying and rumbling, loaded to the brim with boxes and with Red Army soldiers sitting on top of the cargo in pointed helmets, bristling with bayonets in all directions, were ferrying away supplies of gold coins from the storerooms of the People's Commissariat of Finance, as well as enormous cases bearing the inscription: "Caution. Tretiakov Art Gallery." Cars growled as they raced through the city.

The glow of a fire trembled very far away in the sky, and unceasing artillery barrages came from the distance, disturbing the stuffy August darkness.

Close to morning, the many thousands strong Cavalry Army weaved like a snake up Tverskaya and through the entire sleepless city of Moscow, hooves clattering on the pavestones, sweeping everything else from the streets and pressing it into doorways and store windows, pushing out the panes of glass. Pointed crimson hoods dangled on the gray backs of the soldiers, and the sharp points of their pikes stabbed at the sky. The thrashing, howling crowd seemed to come alive when it saw the columns lurching forwards, slicing through the overflowing sea of madness. The crowds on the sidewalks began to howl with hope.

"Long live the cavalry!" cried frenzied women's voices.

"Hurrah!" replied the men.

"They're crushing us!! Crushing!" someone howled.

"Help!" they shouted from the sidewalk.

Boxes of cigarettes, silver coins, and watches began to rain on the columns from the sidewalks; a few women jumped out on the road and, risking life and limb, trudged along with the lines of horsemen, grasping the stirrups and kissing them. The voices of the platoon commanders soared up every so often from among the incessant clattering of hooves:

"Rein in."

Someone was singing a cheery, rollicking song, and faces stared from beneath the cocked crimson hats atop the horses, illuminated by unsteady advertising lights. Every now and again, the lines of horsemen with exposed faces were broken up by strange mounted figures wearing unusual masks with tubes draped over their shoulders and cylinders strapped to their backs. Enormous cistern trucks crawled behind them, with very long sleeves and hoses, just like fire trucks, as well as heavy tanks on caterpillar tracks that crushed the pavestones, sealed firmly and glowing with narrow gun-slots. The mounted columns were also interspersed with trucks encased in gray armor, with similar hoses sticking out and with white skulls painted on the sides next to the inscriptions: "Gas. Volunteer-Chem."

"Save us, fellas!" people howled from the sidewalks. "Smash the snakes… save Moscow!"

Good-natured curses rolled through the ranks. Packs of cigarettes flew through the brightly lit night air, and white teeth flashed from atop the horses at the crazed people. A muffled song was spreading through the ranks, tugging at the heartstrings:

> "…Need neither ace, nor queen, nor jack.
> We'll beat the snakes without a doubt,
> They have no chance, we'll stack the deck…"[1]

---

1 The song is to the tune of *Internationale* (*Ni Dieu, ni César, ni tribun…*).

Rumbling hurrahs reverberated over the human mass, because a rumor had spread through the crowd that the aging,
gray commander of the enormous hulk of cavalry, a legend
from ten years ago, was riding in front of the columns, wearing the same crimson hood as the other riders. The crowd kept
howling and sending a somewhat calming hum of "hurrah…
hurrah…" flying into the sky…

* * *

The institute was dimly lit. News only traveled there in
the form of isolated, hazy, and muffled echoes. Once, a fan-
like burst of gunfire erupted beneath the fiery clock by the
Manege: some looters who had tried to rob an apartment on
Volkhonka had been summarily shot. There were few cars
on the streets, for they were mostly drifting towards the train
stations. In the professor's laboratory, where a single lamp
burned dimly, casting a swirl of light onto the table, Persikov was sitting silently with his head in his hands. Layers of
smoke drifted around him. The ray in the chamber had been
extinguished. The frogs in the terrariums were silent, as they
had already fallen asleep. The professor was not working, and
he was not reading. At his side, beneath his left elbow, lay
yesterday's news telegram column, which said that Smolensk
was engulfed in flames and that artillery units were shelling
the Mozhaisk woods sector by sector in order to destroy deposits of crocodile eggs, which lay in every damp ravine. It
said that the air squadrons near Viazma had had considerable
success after flooding almost the entire district with gas, but
also that human casualties in those regions had been countless due to the fact that the population, instead of evacuat-
ing the districts in an orderly fashion, had panicked and was
dashing every which way in isolated groups, at their own peril.
It said that a special cavalry division from the Caucasus had
won a brilliant victory against ostrich hordes somewhere in
the direction of Mozhaisk, chopping them all to pieces and

destroying enormous deposits of ostrich eggs. The division suffered minimal losses. The government had announced that, if the reptiles were to breach the 150-mile safety zone around the capital, the city would be fully evacuated. Office and factory workers were to remain absolutely calm. The government would take the strictest measures to prevent a repeat of the Smolensk fiasco, where the city caught fire in several places after the people, terrified by a sudden attack of several thousands of rattlesnakes, began a hopeless mass exodus, abandoning their burning stoves. The paper said that Moscow had at least half a year's worth of supplies, and that a Soviet presided over by the Commander in Chief was taking urgent measures to fortify apartments in case it became necessary to battle the reptiles on the streets of the capital, should the Red Armies and the air squadrons fail to halt the advance of the reptiles.

The professor was not reading any of this; he was staring into space with glassed-over eyes and smoking. Two people were in the institute besides him – Pankrat and the housekeeper Maria Stepanovna, who kept bursting into tears and had not slept during the three nights she had spent in the professor's office, after the latter refused to abandon his last remaining extinguished chamber. Now Maria Stepanovna was huddling on the oilcloth couch in a dark corner, silently thinking bitter thoughts and staring at a kettle with tea intended for the professor as it boiled on a tripod stand over a gas burner. The institute was silent, and everything happened unexpectedly.

Loud, hateful screams came from outside suddenly, causing Maria Stepanovna to jump up and shriek. Lights began flashing on the street, and Pankrat's voice came from the vestibule. The professor did not pay much attention to this noise. He raised his head for a moment and muttered: "Listen to them go crazy... what am I going to do now?" And he fell back into a stupor. But his stupor was soon disturbed. The iron doors of the institute, which opened onto Herzen Street, began to rumble horribly, and all the walls shook. Then the solid mirrored windowpane burst in the laboratory next door. Glass in the professor's laboratory rang and spilled out of the window frame, and a gray stone jumped into the window, destroying a glass table. The frogs began to thrash in the terrariums and raised a horrible ruckus. Maria Stepanovna started to scream and dart around. She dashed to the professor and grasped him by the hands, crying: "Run, Vladimir Ipatievich, run." He got up from the revolving chair and, fashioning a hook out of his finger, replied to her, and for a brief moment his eyes took on their former sharp twinkle, reminiscent of the former, inspired Persikov.

"I am not going anywhere," he said. "This is just nonsense, they are thrashing like madmen… And if all of Moscow has gone mad, where will I go? So, please, stop shouting. What have I to do with any of this? Pankrat!" he called out, pushing a button.

He probably wanted Pankrat to put an end to all the commotion, which he never liked. But Pankrat could no longer do anything. The banging ended when the doors of the institute opened, and claps of gunshots came from the distance, and then the entire stone institute was filled with running, screaming, and the sound of breaking glass. Maria Stepanovna latched on to Persikov's sleeve and began to drag him off somewhere, but he freed himself and, still wearing his white coat, walked out into the hallway.

"Well?" he asked. The doors burst open, and the first thing that appeared in the doorway was the back of an officer with a crimson chevron and a star on his left sleeve. He was firing his revolver and backing away from the door even as a furious crowd pushed its way in. Then he dashed past Persikov, shouting:

"Save yourself, professor, there is nothing more I can do."

Maria Stepanovna's scream responded to his words. The officer jumped past Persikov, who stood there like a white statue, and disappeared into the dark, winding hallways on the other side. People came flying out of the doors, howling:

"Get him! Kill him…"

"Global villain!"

"He let the snakes loose!"

Contorted faces and torn clothes began to flicker in the hallways, and someone fired a gun. Sticks appeared. Persikov stepped back a little, closed the door leading to the laboratory, where a terrified Maria Stepanovna was standing on her knees on the floor, and stretched out his arms as if crucified… he did not wish to let the crowd inside, and he shouted irritably:

"This is utter madness… you are acting like wild animals. What do you want?" He howled: "Get out!" and ended with his curt, universally known shout: "Pankrat, throw them out of here."

But Pankrat could no longer throw anyone out. His head smashed, Pankrat lay motionless in the vestibule, trampled and torn to pieces, and more and more of the mob tore past him without heeding the gunshots from the police outside.

A short man on crooked, apelike legs, wearing a torn jacket and a tattered shirt askew on his chest, beat the others to Persikov and split the professor's head open with a terrible blow of his stick. Persikov swayed and began to collapse on his side. His last words were:

"Pankrat… Pankrat…"

The utterly innocent Maria Stepanovna was murdered and torn to pieces in the laboratory. The mob smashed the chamber with the extinguished beam, destroyed the terrariums, killing and trampling the frenzied frogs, shattered the glass tables and the reflectors, and an hour later the institute was ablaze and littered with corpses, surrounded by a line of uniformed men armed with electric revolvers. Fire engines were sucking water from the hydrants, directing streams at all the windows as the long streaks of flames roared from inside.

CHAPTER 12

★

A FROSTY DEUS EX MACHINA

On the night of August 19th, 1928, an unheard-of frost came down, unlike anything within the memory of even the oldest folk. It came down and lasted two days, reaching eighteen degrees below freezing. A frenzied Moscow shut all its windows and doors. Only by the end of the third day did the population realize that the frost had saved the capital and all the countless expanses of land in its dominion that were stricken by the horrible catastrophe of 1928. The Cavalry Army near Mozhaisk, having lost three quarters of its contingent, was on the verge of collapse, and the gas-spraying air squadrons had also failed to halt the filthy reptiles advancing on Moscow in a semicircle from the west, south-west, and south directions.

They were stifled by the frost. The repugnant hordes could not bear two days at eighteen below zero, and when the frost disappeared during the last week of August, leaving only wetness and dampness, leaving moisture in the air, leaving the foliage battered by the unexpected cold, there was no one left to fight. The catastrophe was over. Forests, fields, and boundless swamps were still littered with multicolored eggs, some covered with a strange, alien pattern that Phate, who had disappeared without a trace, had mistaken for dirt, but these eggs were completely harmless. They were dead, the embryos inside were finished.

Untold expanses of land would rot for a long time with the countless corpses of crocodiles and snakes, summoned to life by a mysterious ray born on Herzen Street in the eyes of a genius, but they were no longer dangerous. The infirm creations of hot, putrid tropical swamps had perished in two days, covering the territories of three provinces in horrible stench, decay, and putridity.

For a long time there were epidemics, there were widespread illnesses caused by the corpses of the reptiles and the people, and the army was out in force, no longer armed with gas but with explosives, cisterns of kerosene, and hoses, cleansing the land. The cleansing was completed and everything was over by the spring of 1929.

And in the spring of 1929, Moscow began to dance, shine, and whirl with lights once more, and the motorized coaches shuffled along as before, and the moon hung over the dome of the Church of Christ the Savior, as if suspended by a thread. And in place of the two-story institute that had burned down in August of 1928, a new zoological palace was constructed, to be headed by private docent Ivanov, but Persikov was no more. Never again would anyone lay eyes on the confident curled hook of his finger, no one would ever hear the screechy, croaking voice again. The world continued to talk and write about the ray and the catastrophe of 1928 for a long time, but then the name of Professor Vladimir Ipatievich Persikov was gradually shrouded in fog and faded away, just like the red ray he discovered that April night. As for the ray, no one managed to obtain it again, even though that graceful gentleman, now Professor Pyotr Stepanovich Ivanov, kept trying. The first chamber was destroyed by the raging crowd on the night of Persikov's murder. Three chambers burned down in the Nikol- skoye state farm "Red Ray" during the first battle of the air squadrons with the reptiles, and it proved impossible to re- store them. No matter how simple the combination of lenses with the reflected rays of light, it could not be reproduced de- spite Ivanov's efforts. Evidently, it required something special, something beyond mere knowledge, something possessed by only one man in the whole world – the late Professor Vladimir Ipatievich Persikov.

Moscow, October 1924.

AFTERWORD

★

BULGAKOV'S FATAL NOVEL

The Fatal Eggs carries the distinction of being the only one of Bulgakov's novels to be published in its entirety during the author's lifetime. It is Bulgakov's first major foray into social science fiction, to be followed by *A Dog's Heart* – a longer and arguably more developed novel that would not be published in Russia until as late as 1987. It is also significant as one of the first and only works of early Soviet-era science fiction that does not champion communist ideology. However, in *The Fatal Eggs*, science fiction is a vehicle rather than an end; Bulgakov's trenchant, perceptive, and masterfully satirical observations of the social and ideological fabric of post-revolutionary Soviet society connect his writing with real life in a way few writers can match. At the same time, Bulgakov's focus on universal questions about the ethics of social and scientific advancement, and the roles of power and responsibility, have kept his work relevant and enthralling to this day. And then, of course, there is Bulgakov's legendary literary style, revered by many generations of Russians and continuing to find new admirers elsewhere in the world.

The novel is at least partly inspired by the work of H. G. Wells; in fact, Bulgakov makes a direct mention, at the end of the third chapter, of one of the works that contributed to the plot. Wells's *The Food of the Gods and How It Came to Earth* relates the story of two scientists who discover a substance that can accelerate the growth and increase the size of living organisms, setting the stage for a confrontation between the newly created giants, who view themselves as heralds of progress, and the rest of humanity. And many will notice the parallels between the destruction of the reptiles by the Russian frost (an interesting, if not oddly foreshadowing, denouement for creatures hatched from German eggs) and the death of the alien invaders in *War of the Worlds* due to terrestrial pathogens. It should be mentioned, however, that the original draft of *The Fatal Eggs* is believed to have ended with the reptiles overrunning Moscow. Either pressured by Soviet censorship, or anticipating its objections over such a politically dubious ending, Bulgakov reworked the conclusion along more Wellsian lines.

There is another amusing link to Wells: upon returning from abroad in 1925, Vladimir Mayakovsky mentioned that an American newspaper had printed a story, under the heading "Snake Eggs in Moscow," that related the events of *The Fatal Eggs* as if they had really happened. This is, of course, reminiscent of the 1938 radio broadcast of *War of the Worlds* that many listeners took for a real news report. Some would find this sort of coincidence to be perfectly in line with Bulgakov's mystical reputation, acquired in large part due to his supernatural magnum opus, *The Master and Margarita*.

In *The Fatal Eggs*, Bulgakov had already found his uniquely flowing writing style, and the novel is a testament to his talent of expressing complex things briefly but meaningfully, as well as portraying grim and unsettling events in a humorous, satirical light. But while Bulgakov had already crossed the threshold that would leave him and his writing firmly entrenched in Russian literature and the Russian psyche, *The Fatal Eggs* is generally considered a somewhat less developed and mature work than its successors. For a long time, Bulgakov himself would consider it merely a writing experiment and remain unsure as to what to make of it. On the night of December 28, 1924, he made the following entry in his journal:

> "In the evening, I read my short novel *The Fatal Eggs* at Nikitina's. I went there with a childish desire to distinguish myself and flaunt,

but I left with a complex emotion. What is this work? A topical satire? Or an impudent gesture? Or is it something serious, perhaps? If so, then it is half-baked. In any case, there were about 30 people there, and not only are none of them writers, but no one understands a thing about Russian literature.

"I fear I may get booted to 'places not so distant'[1] for all these heroics of mine."

As the last sentence indicates, however, Bulgakov understood the politically dangerous nature of his work perfectly well. The "impudence" of his social commentary goes beyond the admittedly biting satirical portrayals of Soviet life in the 1920s. Today, *The Fatal Eggs*, where a red ray created by an irresponsible genius and coopted by blind authority breeds an unstoppable generation of ravenous monsters, is widely viewed as an allegory for the revolution and Soviet attempts to establish a new society.

A number of Bulgakov scholars believe the protagonist, Vladimir Ipatievich Persikov, to be at least partly based on Vladimir Ilyich Lenin. The two have similar names, they share a similar appearance and know the same languages, they are of the same age. And just as Persikov experiments with new types of life forms using his red ray, so does Lenin initiate an enormous experiment in Russia beneath the "red ray" of Soviet ideology. The character of Phate, meanwhile, has been linked with Trotsky (in this interpretation, Bulgakov's novel once again takes on a prophetic tone – just as Phate disappeared without a trace shortly after the snakes he bred went out of control, so was Trotsky forced to disappear from Russia in 1929, five years after *The Fatal Eggs* was written, after his former comrades turned on him). Naturally, Lenin and Trotsky

---

1 This expression was born as a Tsarist-era euphemism referring to certain (less severe) destinations for exile and grew into a more general sarcastic reference to imprisonment or deportation.

would not have been the only inspirations for Bulgakov's characters; literary researchers have identified a number of potential candidates that provided various traits for Persikov, Phate, and others, including scientists, political figures, and Bulgakov's acquaintances and family members. Enumerating all these connections is beyond the scope of this writing, but, as a start, the interested reader is invited to seek out the prolific and informative commentary from Bulgakov scholars M. Chudakova, B. Sokolov, L. Yanovskaya, and many others.

In light of these interpretations, the fact that the novel made it past the censorship in the first place is interesting in itself. The novel was likely rescued by the fact that, in 1924, Bulgakov had not yet achieved notoriety with Soviet government and its literary critics, which would effectively put an end to his career as a writer and playwright by the 1930s. B. Sokolov also notes that the censors may have interpreted the reptilian attack on Moscow as a parody of foreign interventionism (the snakes had hatched from foreign eggs, after all), while the chicken plague that sweeps through the land but stops at the borders could have been viewed as symbolizing Soviet revolutionary ideas.

Once published, however, the connotations of Bulgakov's novel did not escape the attention of the critics. Despite a small number of contrasting opinions, as well as privately expressed praise, the majority of the critical reception attacked the novel as an anti-Soviet lampoon, latching on to everything from allegories to Soviet rule to the alleged portrayal of near-future Moscow as a capitalist, "European" city. And the attention of the secret police was not far behind. An informant for the Joint State Political Administration (OGPU) had this to say in a report dated February 22, 1928:

> "One can only wonder at the patience and
> tolerance of the Soviet authorities, which have
> still not banned the circulation of Bulgakov's
> book *The Fatal Eggs* (pub. in *Nedra*). This book

represents a most brazen and outrageous slander of the Red government. It describes vividly how a red ray gives birth to snakes which devour each other and then advance on Moscow. There is also a foul section – a malicious nod at the late comrade Lenin – where a dead toad retains a sinister expression on its face even after dying.

"How this book continues to circulate freely is impossible to fathom. People are reading it avidly. Young people love Bulgakov, he is popular."

By the time of the above report, the so-called patience and tolerance of the Soviet authorities had already caught up with Bulgakov. *A Dog's Heart*, the tale of a scientist who transforms a dog into a human being only to discover that he has created a monster, did not receive exposure beyond isolated readings in the same literary clubs where Bulgakov had read *The Fatal Eggs*. An OGPU agent present at one such reading denounced the novel and predicted that it would not see the light of day. Bulgakov's masterpiece, *The Master and Margarita*, would likewise remain hidden until long after the author's death.

It is unclear how much of the blame should be assigned to *The Fatal Eggs* in particular, but its publication certainly drew attention to Bulgakov (in the end, of course, it was not a matter of "if" but "when"). After its publication, the vilification of Bulgakov by critics would continue and intensify; his novels and plays would be routinely banned by higher authorities, frequently leaving him without any source of income; his anguish and depression at seeing all avenues of artistic expression closed to him may have accelerated the decline of his health until his death in 1940 from a hereditary kidney ailment. Although the brilliant professors in Bulgakov's works had performed far greater scientific miracles, dialysis and kidney transplants would not be performed for several more years.

The gradual thaw that began after Stalin's death would eventually reveal Bulgakov's work to the world, establishing him as one of the most significant literary figures of the 20th century. The final, and perhaps the most ironic and bittersweet twist that will be mentioned here is this: today, there are far more people in Russia, and in the rest of the world, who can recognize and describe Professor Persikov than there are people who can recognize and describe the OGPU informants who denounced Bulgakov, the loyal Soviet critics who hounded and tormented him throughout his life, or many of the party leaders who managed to delay, though not prevent, his works from reaching a grateful audience.

Also from Translit Publishing

THE TALE OF
HODJA NASREDDIN:
DISTURBER OF THE PEACE

by Leonid Solovyov

Print edition
ISBN: 978-0-9812695-0-4

E-book and Kindle
ISBN: 978-0-9812695-1-1

Returning to Bukhara after a long exile, Hodja Nasreddin finds his family gone, his home destroyed, and his city in the grasp of corrupt and greedy rulers who have brought pain and suffering upon the common folk. But Hodja Nasreddin is not one to bow to oppression or abandon the downtrodden. Though he is armed only with his quick wits and his donkey, all the swords, walls, and dungeons in the land cannot stop him!

Leaning on his own experiences and travels during the first half of the 20th century, Leonid Solovyov weaves the many stories and anecdotes about Hodja Nasreddin – a legendary folk character in the Middle East and Central Asia – into a masterful tale brimming with passionate love for life, liberty, and happiness. Discover a hidden gem of Russian literature!

CPSIA information can be obtained
at www.ICGtesting.com
Printed in the USA
LVHW041508260123
737941LV00002B/253

9 780981 269528